She looked up and found him looking down at her. Even in the semidarkness, she could see the heat in his eyes.

He offered nothing but comfort, but the heat was there between them anyway.

She didn't look away.

And then, in the blink of an eye, somehow everything changed. Slowly, giving her plenty of time to protest, he lowered his lips and brushed them over hers.

Oh, wow. Was this really happening?

That Moses Mann would be kissing her seemed surreal on some level. He was so...strong and brave and a millionaire and worldly—everything she wasn't. She was just a plain country girl.

They were so completely wrong for each other. Unfortunately, her hormones didn't give a damn. Need punched into her like never before, something big and scary and overpowering and completely unexpected.

MOST ELIGIBLE SPY

DANA MARTON

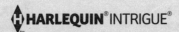
HARLEQUIN® INTRIGUE®

Recycling programs for this product may not exist in your area.

With many thanks to my wonderful editor, Allison Lyons. Thank you so much Deb Posey Chudzinski, Lisa Boggs, Amanda Scott, Maureen Miller, Valerie Earnshaw and all my wonderful friends who support me online.

ISBN-13: 978-0-373-69715-1

MOST ELIGIBLE SPY

HARLEQUIN®
www.Harlequin.com

Printed in U.S.A.

ABOUT THE AUTHOR

Dana Marton is the author of more than a dozen fast-paced, action adventure, romantic-suspense novels and a winner of a Daphne du Maurier Award of Excellence. She loves writing books of international intrigue, filled with dangerous plots that try her tough-as-nails heroes and the special women they fall in love with. Her books have been published in seven languages in eleven countries around the world. When not writing or reading, she loves to browse antiques shops and enjoys working in her sizable flower garden, where she searches for "bad" bugs with the skills of a superspy and vanquishes them with the agility of a commando soldier. Every day in her garden is a thriller. To find more information on her books, please visit www.danamarton.com. She loves to hear from her readers and can be reached via email at danamarton@danamarton.com.

Books by Dana Marton

HARLEQUIN INTRIGUE

933—BRIDAL OP
962—UNDERCOVER SHEIK
985—SECRET CONTRACT*
991—IRONCLAD COVER*
1007—MY BODYGUARD*
1013—INTIMATE DETAILS*
1039—SHEIK SEDUCTION
1055—72 HOURS
1085—SHEIK PROTECTOR
1105—TALL, DARK AND LETHAL
1121—DESERT ICE DADDY
1136—SAVED BY THE MONARCH*
1142—ROYAL PROTOCOL*
1179—THE SOCIALITE AND THE BODYGUARD
1206—STRANDED WITH THE PRINCE**
1212—ROYAL CAPTIVE**
1235—THE SPY WHO SAVED CHRISTMAS
1299—THE BLACK SHEEP SHEIK
1328—LAST SPY STANDING
1358—SPY HARD
1364—THE SPY WORE SPURS
1448—MOST ELIGIBLE SPY‡

*Mission: Redemption
**Defending the Crown
‡HQ: Texas

CAST OF CHARACTERS

Molly Rogers—A single mom, mourning her brother who is accused of a slew of crimes. Does the man interrogating her want to frame her? Or is he the only one standing between her and a band of ruthless criminals?

Moses Mann—Member of a top-secret commando group (SDDU). He is on the Texas border to stop terrorists from coming into the country, then will move on to his next assignment. But will Molly Rogers change his plans?

Sheriff Shane—The Hullett, Texas, sheriff. There are clues pointing to his possible involvement in smuggling.

Sheriff Davis—He's the sheriff of the next small town, the one person actually believing Molly and supporting her. Yet Mo has his suspicions of the man. But is he biased because of jealousy?

SDDU—Special Designation Defense Unit. A top-secret commando team established to fight terrorism and other international crime that affects the U.S. The group's existence is known only by a select few. Members are recruited from the best of the best.

Chapter One

She had that Earth Mother kind of natural feminine beauty, the type of woman who belonged at a bake sale or a PTA meeting, not in an interrogation room on the Texas border. Then again, smugglers came in all shapes and sizes.

Dressed in mom jeans and a simple T-shirt—a crew neck, so there wasn't even a hint of cleavage—she wore precious little makeup. Her chestnut hair hung in a simple ponytail, no highlights, nothing fancy. She did her best to look and sound innocent.

Moses Mann, undercover special commando, did his best not to fall for the act. "Let's try it again, and go for the truth this time."

If all her wholesome goodness swayed him, he was professional enough not to show it as he questioned her. He wasn't in the small, airless interrogation room in the back of an office trailer to appreciate Molly Rogers's curves. He was here to pry into her deepest secrets.

"When did you first suspect that your brother, Dylan Rogers, was involved in illegal activities?"

The smell of her shampoo, something old-fashioned like lemon verbena, filled the air and tickled Mo's nose. He kept his face impassive as he leaned back in his metal folding chair and looked across the desk at her.

Anger flared in her green eyes. "My brother didn't do

anything illegal," she said in a measured tone. "Someone framed him."

Mo's gaze dropped to her round breasts that suddenly lifted toward him as she pulled her spine even straighter. He caught himself. Blinked. "Your brother was a cold-blooded killer."

He'd personally seen the carnage at the old cabin on the Texas–Mexico border not far from here, the blood-soaked floorboards and the pile of bodies. He'd been the one who'd taken to the hospital the two children Dylan had kidnapped to sell into the adoption black market. Dylan had ended up with a bullet in the head during the takedown—well deserved as far as Mo was concerned.

He didn't have much sympathy for the man's sister, either. "Have you ever helped him smuggle illegal immigrants into the country? Drugs? Weapons?"

Her jaw worked with restrained anger. She clutched her hands tightly in front of her. The nicks and red spots on her fingers said she saw her share of farm chores and housework on a daily basis. Her full lips narrowed, but somehow remained sensuous.

"Let me tell you something about my brother. He stood by me all my life. By me and my son. I don't know if we'd be alive at this stage without him." She stuck out her chin. "He was a good man."

Her absolute loyalty to family was commendable, even if misguided. Mo waited a beat, giving her time to calm a little before he said, "People are multidimensional. The face he showed you might not be the face he showed to others."

For the four men he'd killed at the Cordero ranch, Dylan Rogers had been the face of death, in fact. And he would have killed Grace Cordero, his neighbor, too, if not for Ryder, Mo's teammate, who'd arrived just in time to save Grace and those two kids.

Dylan Rogers had been a dark-hearted criminal. And the crimes he was publicly accused of paled in comparison to the one Mo couldn't even mention. Dylan was likely connected to people who planned on smuggling terrorists into the country—the true target of Mo's six-man undercover team.

As far as the locals were concerned, the team—all seasoned commando—were working with CBP, Customs and Border Protection. They'd come to survey the smuggling situation and investigate recent cases so they could come up with budget recommendations for policy makers. A fairly decent cover while they did their counterterrorism work without anyone being the wiser.

Smuggling was big business in the borderlands, sometimes even with customs or police officers on the bad guys' payroll. His team gathered information from local law enforcement, but shared nothing. They trusted no one at this stage. They kept to themselves while gathering every clue, following every lead. And one of their best leads right now was Molly Rogers.

But instead of cooperating, she was looking at the time on her phone in front of her. She bit her bottom lip.

"In a hurry?"

She nodded.

Too damn bad. "If you want to leave, you need to start talking." Mo tapped his pen on the desk between them. "Are there any illegal activities going on at your ranch at this time, Miss Rogers?"

"No. I already told you." She glanced at the phone again. "How long are you going to keep me here? If you're not charging me with anything, you have to let me go. I know my rights."

He regarded her dispassionately.

She had no idea how quickly a "terror suspect" designation could strip away all her precious rights. He'd seen people go into the system with that tag and disappear for a good long time, sometimes forever. If her brother's smuggling career included terrorist contacts… If she knew about it…

Her brother was dead, beyond questioning. Without information from her, Mo's team sat without a paddle, trapped on the proverbial creek, with the rapids quickly approaching.

She squirmed in her seat. "I have to go home to meet the school bus."

Her weak point. He was about to get to that.

He patted his shirt pocket, pretending to look for something. "I can arrange for someone to pick up your son. I have a card here somewhere for Social Services."

All the blood ran out of her face as she caught the veiled threat. She was a single mother without family. If they took her into custody, her son would go to foster care.

"I don't know anything about any illegal business," she rushed to say. "I swear. Please."

He liked her pleading tone. Progress. He'd scared her at last. He'd done far worse before to gain usable intelligence from the enemy. He'd done things that would shock her.

He pushed his chair back and stood. "I'm going to step out for a minute. Why don't you give some thought to how you really want to play this? For your son's sake."

"I'm not playing."

He didn't respond. He didn't even turn. He simply walked out and closed the door behind him.

Jamie Cassidy, the operations coordinator, sat at his computer in the main part of the office the team shared. He looked up for a second. "Singing like a bird in there?"

"I wish. She says she doesn't know anything."

"Do you believe her?"

Mo considered that for a moment, recalling every word she'd said, adding to that her body language and all the visual clues, and the depth of his experience. He didn't like what he came up with. He wanted her to be guilty. It would have made everything much easier.

He shrugged. "Bottom line is, we have nothing to hold her on." Maybe her brother did keep her in the dark about his smuggling. Either that, or she was an award-worthy actress.

"You gonna push her harder?"

He could have. "Not today."

Not because he felt that stupid attraction, but because of her son. Whatever she did or didn't know about smuggling, her son was innocent, and Mo wasn't ready to turn the kid's life upside down until he had damned good reason.

The boy had just lost his uncle. He didn't need to come home from school and search through an empty house, wondering what happened to his mother.

"You got anything?"

Jamie shook his head. "Shep just checked in. Everything's quiet, he says."

Shep and Ray were patrolling the border, Ray's leg still in a cast, but well enough for a ride along. Ryder, the team leader, was off tying up loose ends with a human-smuggling ring the team had recently busted. With what stood at stake, the six-man team wasn't about to leave any stones unturned. They pushed and pushed, and then they pushed harder.

"Keith called in, too," Jamie said. "He's getting frustrated over there." Keith was across the border, doing undercover surveillance to identify the local players on that side.

"He's young. He'll learn patience." Not that Mo felt any

at the moment. "Once we have our third man, we'll have our link."

From what they'd gathered so far, three men coordinated most of the smuggling activities on this side of the border. They'd gotten two. Dylan Rogers had been shot, unfortunately, before he could be questioned. Mikey Metzner, a local business owner closely tied to human smuggling, was in custody, but seemed to be the lowest ranking of the three, and without any direct knowledge of the big boss in Mexico.

"The third guy is the key." Even if he hadn't been the link to the big boss before, he was now.

"We'll get him."

Mo nodded then turned and walked back into the interrogation room.

"I can't tell you something I don't know about," Molly Rogers said immediately. "Look, I think you're wrong about my brother. This is not fair. I—"

"We're done for today. I'll take you home." He'd picked her up earlier, so she didn't have her car.

He held the door open for her, and she gave him as wide a berth as possible as she passed by him, clutching her purse to her chest. The top of her head didn't quite reach his chin. About five-four, no taller than that, and curvy in just the right places and... Mo tried not to notice her enticing figure or the way her soft chestnut ponytail swung as she hurried ahead of him.

Jamie caught him looking and raised an eyebrow.

He ignored him as he led her through the office, then scanned his ID card and pushed the entry door open. Outside, the South Texas heat hit them like a punch in the face.

His black SUV waited up front on the gravel. "Better give it a minute to let the hot air out." He opened the doors, reached in and turned the air conditioner on the highest setting.

Renting office space in Hullett's business district would have been more comfortable, would have come with climate-controlled parking. But from a tactical standpoint, the trailer office by the side of the road in the middle of nowhere made more sense for his team.

They could see for miles without obstacles, had complete control over the premises. They didn't expect an attack, but if anything did happen, the Kevlar-reinforced trailer with its bulletproof windows was a hell of a lot more defensible than a run-of-the-mill rented office. In his job, practicalities always came before niceties.

He gave the AC another few seconds then slipped into his seat and waited until she did the same on the other side.

"Thank you for believing me," she said, her faint, citrusy scent filling his car.

He raised an eyebrow. "Don't get ahead of yourself. We're not done here. We're just taking a break."

He let her sit and stew for the first five minutes of the drive down the dusty country road before he started in on her again, gentling his voice, switching to the "good cop" part of the routine.

"Anything you tell me can only help your case. If you got dragged into something against your will… Things like that happen. The important thing now is to come clean. We need your help here."

Her posture stiffened. "Am I an official suspect?"

"A person of interest," he told her after a few seconds.

And when she paled, he found that he didn't like making her miserable. But he would, if the job called for it.

The op was too important to let something like basic attraction mess with his focus. She was the wrong woman at the wrong time for him to get interested in. Even beyond the op. He planned on this being his last job with the SDDU, Special Designation Defense Unit, an undercover commando team that did everything from intelligence gathering abroad to hostage rescue to counterterrorism work.

His focus was on his mission and nothing else. He could ignore the tingles he felt in the pit of his stomach every time he looked at the woman next to him. If he did well here, his CIA transfer was as good as approved. Molly Rogers wasn't going to mess that up for him.

THE CAR FLEW down the road, Molly's stomach still so clenched from the interrogation she thought she might throw up. She took in the fancy dashboard, covered with computer displays, radio units, radar and other things she'd never seen before. She so wasn't going to feel guilty if she ruined any of that.

"When do you think I can claim my brother's personal effects?"

All she wanted was to put all this behind her, for her brother's name to be cleared. And an official apology in the local paper. Dylan didn't deserve to be dragged through the mud like this.

But instead of law enforcement investigating how and why Dylan had been framed, they kept on with their idiotic suspicions about him, even dragging her into the mess.

The man next to her kept his eyes on the road. "For now your brother's personal possessions are evidence in a multiple murder case."

"The sheriff won't let me into Dylan's apartment in Hullett, either." Everyone seemed to be against her these days.

"They need to get everything processed."

She hated Moses Mann. He had zero sympathy for her or her situation. He was twice her size and had used that in the interrogation room to intimidate her. He was missing half an eyebrow, which made him look pretty fierce. His muscles were just on this side of truly scary. She had a feeling he knew how to use his strength and use it well.

If he had a softer—reasonable—side, she sure hadn't seen it. He'd called her brother a conscienceless criminal and pretty much accused her of being the same. He threatened her with Social Services.

Her stomach clenched.

The day she saw Moses Mann for the last time would be a good day. He made her nervous and scared and so self-aware it bordered on painful. She had to watch every move, every word, lest he read something criminal into it. She looked away from him.

The land stretched flat and dry all around them as far as the eye could see. He drove the dusty country road in silence for a while before he resumed questioning her, asking her some of the same questions he'd asked before. She gave him the same answers. He was still trying to trip her when they reached her road at last.

Thank God. Another ten minutes and she would have been ready to jump from the moving car.

He parked his SUV at the end of her driveway, and she was out before he shut the engine off. Her dogs charged from behind the house, Max and Cocoa in the lead, Skipper in the back, all three of them country mutts from the pound.

They greeted her first.

"No jumping." She pushed Max down then scratched behind his ear.

He kept jumping anyway. Skipper barked, running around her in circles. They were worked up over something.

They checked out the man by her side next, tails wagging. They were about the three friendliest, goofiest guard dogs in Texas, trained to be nice to everyone, since her son often had friends over.

"Be nice," she said anyway, even if she wouldn't have been too put out if one of them peed on Moses Mann's combat boots. Not that she was vengeful or anything.

But the dogs were doing their best to crowd each other out as the man gave them some ear scratching. They seemed to think they'd found a new best friend. Figured.

He looked as if he enjoyed the attention. "There you go. That's a good dog."

She hoped he'd at least get fleas.

He gave a few final pats as he looked at her.

She cleared her throat. "Thanks for the ride." *Hint, hint. Go away.*

She didn't like the relaxed smile he'd gotten from playing with her traitor dogs. It made him look more human than soldier machine. If she began to think of him as anything other than "the enemy," he'd try to trick her into a false confession or something. Since they couldn't do anything more to her brother now, he and his team would probably do anything to ruin her life instead. She couldn't afford to let her guard down for a minute.

She waited for him to get back into his car and drive away. She didn't want him following her into the house, so she went to check the mailbox, playing for time, and bit her lip as she opened the flap door, her hand hesitating.

"What's wrong?" he called over.

How on earth had he caught that half-second pause? "Nothing."

She thrust her hand forward and grabbed the stack of envelopes. *Everything.* Bills scared her these days. She'd received a mortgage check the day before, for the ranch that she'd thought had been long free and clear. Dylan had taken out a new mortgage, apparently.

Which didn't mean he was a bad brother. Or a murderer.

He'd worked so hard, had so much on his mind... He'd simply forgotten to tell her.

She kept her back to Moses Mann. "Just making sure there aren't any wasps in there. They keep trying to move in." Also true. She's had a lot of trouble with wasps this year.

She shuffled through the envelopes, then relaxed. No unexpected bills, thank God. The new mortgage was more than she could handle.

Her cell phone rang and she glanced at the display. The agent from Brandsom Mining. The man had a sixth sense for knowing when she felt desperate. But not that desperate yet. She pushed the off button.

"Who was that?"

She wasn't going to discuss her problems with Moses Mann. He would have no qualms about using any weakness against her. "Telemarketer," she said. Sounded better than *People who are trying to take the ranch away from me*.

The land had some collapsed mine shafts left over from its old coal mining days. The mine had run dry and had been abandoned in her grandfather's time. But Brandsom Mining wanted to buy the ranch for exploration, thought that with modern methods of surface mining they might be able to get something out of the place.

And ruin the land in the process, mess up the water tables, have heavy machinery tear up the earth. No thanks. Dylan and she had always been in full agreement about that. The ranch was her son's inheritance. The Rogers Ranch would stay in Rogers hands until there was no longer a Rogers left.

She glanced at her phone. "Bus should be coming in a minute." *Feel free to leave now.*

But the guy seemed impervious to hints.

Her heart lifted at the sight of the school bus coming

around the bend, its old engine laboring. She glanced at the major pain at her side, wishing he would disappear. If he stayed, Logan would be asking questions about him. But the man was looking at her pickup, his attention 100 percent focused there as the bus stopped and Logan ran down the steps.

For a second she forgot about Moses Mann as she caught her son up into her arms and held him tight. The dogs were jumping all over them, muscling their way in with enthusiasm.

Logan squirmed. "Mo-om, not in front of the other kids."

She let him go with a half smile. Right. He was a big kid now, supposedly, eight years old. She made sure not to take his hand, or offer to carry his bag as she turned toward the house. But she did say "I missed you, buddy" as the school bus pulled away.

Moses Mann was walking over, his cell phone in hand. "I need you to go sit in my car."

Her muscles clenched at the hard expression on his face and the silent warning in his eyes. "What's going on?"

"Just for a few minutes."

If she were alone, she would have demanded an explanation. But she didn't want to get into an argument with the man in front of Logan. Because he *could* make her sit in his car. He *could* take her right back with him. She didn't want things to get worse than they were. Which meant she'd do as he asked. For the time being.

She swallowed and reached for her son's hand, big kid or not. "This nice gentleman is Mr. Mann." She did her best to sound normal. "He has a really cool car. Want to check it out?"

"Hi, Mr. Mann. Can I sit in the front?"

He nodded with an encouraging smile, the first she'd seen on him. "Just don't turn on the siren."

Logan's eyes went wide, a big smile stretching his face. "You have a siren? Is it like an undercover police car?"

"Kind of."

"Are you going to find the bad men who hurt Uncle Dylan?"

He hesitated for a second, his gaze cutting to her, before he said, "I'm working on that situation."

Logan sprinted for the car and she walked after him, the streaks of dirt on his back catching her eye.

"What happened to your shirt?"

He froze and looked at his feet. "Nothing."

"Logan?"

He turned but wouldn't look at her. "It's no big deal, Mom."

Her heart sank. She didn't have to ask what the fight was about. He'd been teased again with what the papers said about his uncle. "What do we always say about fighting?"

He hung his head and mumbled, "The best way to win a fight is to walk away from it."

She caught Mo watching them. He didn't look like the type who walked away from a fight. Well, that was his problem. "All right. Let's get in the car. We'll talk about this later."

When she was behind the wheel, Mo started toward her house. But then he stopped and motioned her to roll the window down, tossed her his keys. "Lock yourselves in." He fixed her with a stern look. "And if there's any trouble, you drive away."

THE DOGS STAYED by the car, whining to get in. They wanted to play with the kid. Good. Better to have them out of his way. Mo dialed his phone, keeping his focus on the house's windows as he approached.

The two-story ranch house was well kept, had a new roof. A row of yellow roses trimmed the wraparound porch that held half a dozen rockers. He dashed across the distance to the steps just as Jamie picked up his call on the other end. "I'm at the Rogers ranch. I need a crime-scene kit."

"You better not be having fun out there while I'm filing reports at the office."

"Molly Rogers's tires were slashed. In the past three hours. Everything was fine when I picked her up earlier."

"You need backup? Ryder just came in."

Ryder had recently been appointed team leader when the powers that be made the SDDU's Texas headquarters permanent. The top secret commando unit mostly worked international missions, infiltration, hostage rescue, search and destroy, espionage and the like.

But when a terrorist threat had been indicated for this section of the border, the Colonel sent a small team in. They'd come for this specific mission, but there was enough going on in the border region that the Colonel decided to make the team here permanent.

"If you can bring the kit, that should be enough." Mo pushed the screen door open as he reached for his gun, then opened the entry door with a simple twist of his wrist and scowled. Hardly anyone kept their houses locked around here. He didn't understand that kind of blind faith in humanity, not after all he'd seen.

"I think whoever messed with the tires is gone." The dogs hadn't signaled an intruder. "But I'm going to check out the place anyway." He closed the phone and slipped it into his back pocket.

He started with the kitchen. He'd been in here before,

with a search warrant and his team, after Dylan's death. They'd found nothing usable then and he didn't bother to look for any incriminating evidence now, just for possible danger. He checked the gun cabinet in the hall closet—full of hunting rifles. Locked. Nothing seemed missing.

He moved through room by room. The bathroom at the top of the stairs still held the faint scent of Molly Rogers's shampoo, everything in its place, everything spotlessly clean.

A little more disorder in the boy's room, a dozen toy soldiers scattered on the floor. But the next room over, her bedroom, was immaculate. He scanned the old-fashioned antique four-poster bed, feminine and delicate.

Would probably break under his weight— He caught the thought. He didn't need to think about himself in Molly Rogers's bed.

But he couldn't help noticing the strappy nightgown that peeked from under the cover. He forced his gaze past the lavender silk after a long moment.

He checked the next two small rooms, including the closets, found no signs that anyone had been in the house. He put his gun away and plodded down the stairs. In the kitchen, he pulled out a business card with his cell-phone number and stuck it on the fridge with a magnet decorated with elbow macaroni, probably made by Logan. Then he strode down the driveway, told them to get out of the car.

He turned to the boy first. "I need to talk to your mom for a second."

Logan looked at his mother.

"Why don't you go play some video games?" she suggested.

He grinned as wide as a grin could go and ran up to the house, his backpack bobbing, the dogs following him. He glanced back and yelled, "Goodbye, Mr. Mann."

He lifted a hand in a wave. Seemed like a well-raised kid.

"What did he get into a fight over?" he asked when the boy had passed out of hearing distance.

"Kids have been picking on him this last couple of weeks because of what they'd heard about his uncle." She shot him a glare as if it was all his fault. "Usually he's pretty good at walking away, but he really idolized my brother."

Whatever Dylan Rogers had done, someone beating on the kid for it didn't sit well with Mo. "You can't always walk away from trouble. I could teach him how to defend himself."

"Absolutely not. I'll handle my son's problems." She crossed her arms. "What were you doing in my house?"

Mo rolled his shoulders. She was right. Her son was none of his business, had nothing whatsoever to do with his op. Getting personally involved would have been a bad idea. *Back to business.* He gestured her over to her pickup and pointed at the slashed tires, watching for her reaction.

She stared, her jaw tightening. For a second he thought he might have seen moisture in the corner of one eye as her gaze filled with misery. "I can't afford new tires."

Money was the least of her problems. "We'll be taking some fingerprints." He gave her a hard look. "I want you to keep your doors locked. Car doors, house doors, garage door, the works. Do you know how to shoot any of those guns in the gun cabinet?"

She drew her gaze from the tires at last. "I might be a pacifist, but I'm still a Texan."

He watched her, trying to puzzle her out. Back in the interrogation room, his threat of calling Social Services had scared her. The slashed tires hadn't, just annoyed her. He liked that she was brave, but he wanted her to be careful. "I left my number on your fridge. Call me if you need me for anything. Don't take this lightly."

She looked back at the tires. "Why would somebody do this to me?"

He had a fair idea. "Maybe one of your brother's friends saw me pick you up. This could be a warning to make sure you don't tell any secrets." He paused for emphasis. "We could protect you and your son. If you were to cooperate."

Instead of jumping on that offer, her muscles only tightened another notch, true anger coming into her eyes.

"Quit blackmailing me with my son. I don't know any secrets. Goodbye, Mr. Mann." Then she turned on her heels and marched up to the house, hips swinging. She let the screen door slam shut behind her.

He would have lied if he said all that fire didn't draw him in, at least a little.

To distract himself from that thought, he checked the outbuildings while he waited for Jamie. Not a single door locked, barn, stables, shed, all the outbuildings open. But he found no signs of damage inside any of them. If the tire slasher had gone through, he hadn't messed with anything else.

As he stepped back outside, he scanned the endless fields around the buildings, not another house in sight. He made a mental note to check on the status of Dylan Rogers's bachelor pad when he got back to the office. Molly and her son would be better off moving there, into town, for the time being.

Not that keeping her safe was his job. For all he knew, she was guilty as sin. But her kid didn't deserve to be in the middle of all this bad business.

There was an amazing connection between mother and son, love and affection, obvious from even their brief encounter. Had he ever had that? Not with his birth mother, for sure. And as his foster mother had died so early, he remembered very little of her.

"How is it that you get both the girl and the action, while I'm stuck in the office?" Jamie's arrival ended the trip down memory lane.

"You're here now."

He looked around. "Sounded more exciting over the phone. Didn't find anyone here?" He sounded disappointed at the missed opportunity for a scuffle.

His steps were sure as he brought the crime-scene kit over to the pickup, but he had a slightly uneven gait. Both of his legs were missing, courtesy of a rough overseas mission that had ended badly. He walked with the aid of two space-age technology prostheses, well hidden under his black cargo pants, originally developed for Olympic athletes.

He looked over the damage carefully. "Find anything else beyond the slashed tires?"

"Nothing."

While Jamie lifted prints, Mo dabbed the tires around the slashes with oversize cotton swabs and sealed those into evidence bags.

Jamie put away the prints he'd collected. "Could be a warning for her to keep quiet about her brother's dealings."

"That was my first thought."

She had no idea how out of her depth she was in all this. He looked toward the house, not liking that he was beginning to feel protective toward Molly Rogers and her son. That could become a problem.

"She's a person of interest in the investigation," he said out loud to remind himself of the exact nature of their relationship.

Maybe if he kept telling himself that was why he was so interested in her, eventually he'd believe it.

His phone rang at the same time as Jamie's. They clicked into a conference call with Ryder.

"Hey, Shep just called. He found some chopped-off fingers. No body to go with them," their team leader said on the other end.

"Where?" Mo tensed, pretty much expecting that he wasn't going to like the answer. He was right about that.

"Rogers land," Ryder said.

Chapter Two

"Anyone call from the lab?" Mo asked as he strode into the office, hating how the days ticked by without any serious progress. They needed a break and soon.

"None." Shep was busy at work at his desk. "Found the damn fingers four days ago. You'd think we'd have something by now." His face was stamped with frustration. "How was surveillance?"

"Hot." He wiped his forehead, enjoying the icy blast of air-conditioning after the hundred-degree heat out there on the border.

The terrain was rough enough so he couldn't drive his SUV up every ridge and down into every gully, which meant he spent half his time hiking, looking for footprints or any other sign of smuggling. He was hoping to catch some mules who could lead him to the man who handled all the dirty business on the U.S. side of the border. So far, he hadn't succeeded.

"Didn't see much. Busting Dylan Rogers slowed business to a trickle. I'm guessing his people are lying low. They figured out they're being watched."

"They'll start up again. They won't want to lose too much money."

"We'll be ready for them." Still, it didn't change the

fact that the team was having a spectacularly unproductive week, chasing down leads that all came to dead ends.

They hadn't been able to dig up anything new on Molly Rogers, either. They had no way to link the three chopped-off fingers to her. She claimed it had been months since she'd been out to the south border of her land. Mo hadn't told her about the fingers. The details of their investigation were strictly on a need-to-know basis.

His instincts said she was innocent. But since images of her wearing that lavender silk nightgown kept popping into his head at every unguarded moment, he wasn't about to trust his instincts on this one.

A small cardboard box sat on his desk. "What's this?"

"New batch of gadgets for testing. More sensitive sensors, longer-radius listening device, long-distance trackers. Pretty cool, actually."

He flipped open the box. Being able to test the latest spy gadgets was part of the perks of the job. But his phone rang before he could truly dig in. He picked it up as soon as he glanced at the display. He'd been waiting for this call all week.

"We have some matches for the prints you got off those slashed tires," Doug, a lab tech from the main office in Washington, said on the other end. "Dylan Rogers, Molly Rogers and a set of unidentified kid prints."

Logan's, he thought as frustration swept through him. "Nothing else?" All he wanted was one small lead, dammit.

"The tire swab samples had human blood in them. Preliminary DNA test links the blood to a murder victim in San Antonio. Garcia Cruz."

He shoved the box aside and sat up straighter. "Meaning the guy was killed with the same knife that slashed those tires?"

"Looks like it."

Garcia Cruz. The name sounded familiar. He brought up the law-enforcement database and did a quick search. The muscles in his jaw tightened as he read.

The Cruz murder had been a gang slaying.

Exactly the wrong type of people for Molly Rogers to get tangled up with.

"And the fingers?" he asked.

"I ran the fingerprints. Another gangbanger. He has a prior record and a long list of aliases. I'll write up a full report and send it over. Just thought I'd give you a heads-up."

"I appreciate that." Mo swore under his breath. Sounded as if it was time to visit Molly Rogers again.

THE DOGS WERE GOING MAD, barking and running around in the yard, then rushing up to her and pulling on her apron.

"I don't have time to play, sorry, guys. I'm way behind." Molly hustled on with her buckets.

Normally she fed the animals before she put Logan on the school bus in the morning, but they'd overslept. The power had gone out sometime in the night and reset the alarm clock. Thank God it was Friday. On Fridays she only had two deliveries, just a few boxes of produce to a local restaurant, and then the milk, both later in the day. She might catch up yet.

The horses were restless, too, snorting at her with reproach as she entered the stables.

"I know, I know. I'm late. Sorry." And she was, even if she *had* needed the sleep.

She'd been way too stressed since her encounter with Moses Mann at the beginning of the week. He didn't seem like the type of man who would just give up and go away.

Every time a car drove by, she expected it to be him, coming to arrest her on some trumped-up charge.

She doled out the feed, then the water to the impatient horses. She patted Paulie, an old gelding. "There. See? Nobody starved."

She moved on to her four cows next and milked them by hand before she let them out to pasture. She carried the five-gallon buckets into one of the outbuildings and got the milk ready for driving it into town. She milked morning and evening, sold the raw milk to an artisan cheese maker in Hullett.

Skipper, Max and Cocoa followed her everywhere, "helping." She took turns pushing the dogs out of the way. "Remind me to schedule your shots." Which brought Grace Cordero to mind. Her once best friend had recently left the army and opened up a vet practice down the road. The Cordero ranch was the closest house to her.

Except Molly hadn't talked to Grace since before Dylan's death.

Grace had been there when Dylan had been shot. She'd said Dylan had kidnapped her.... Why would she say that?

That terrible ache bubbled up in Molly's heart again, so she pushed those thoughts away and refocused on her chores. She let out the chickens from the coop and fed them. The dogs weren't allowed in the fenced-off area that protected her chickens from foxes and coyotes. She shooed them off. Dylan had some booby traps set up for anything that might go after her poultry. The dogs knew the traps and had been trained to stay away, but she didn't like them back here.

"Go play." She pushed them away, and they did run off.

Soon they were barking by the shed. What on earth was wrong with them today? Maybe they sensed a storm coming. She glanced up at the sky, but the clear blue dome stretched from horizon to horizon without a blemish. Looked as if the relentless heat would be staying. Wildfires were more of a threat than a storm at this point.

She collected the eggs into the empty bowl she'd brought the wheat in for the hens. Barely anything. The hens didn't lay much in this kind of heat. She took the eggs into the house, then went back out to look in on her sizable vegetable garden. Weeds never took a break. She didn't use pesticides or herbicides; all her fruits and vegetables were 100 percent organic, which got her top dollar at the local restaurants where she did weekly deliveries.

Since it hadn't rained in forever, watering came first. She decided to use some compost tea as well, so she headed to the shed. The dogs were still scratching at the door. She shooed them away, but when she stepped inside, they rushed past her, nearly pushing her over.

They were growling and sniffing at everything.

"What's up with you today?"

But then she caught it, too. Something was off. Okay, a lot of things were off, she realized suddenly, noticing that her buckets had been pushed around. A couple of the floorboards were damaged.

"All right. What got in this time?" She let the dogs investigate, stepping aside and leaving the door clear in case a wild animal was hiding in some corner and was about to make a dash for freedom.

Despite her best efforts and the dogs, wild critters had a way of getting into her garden and outbuildings from time to time. On the rare occasion, they'd done pretty spectacular damage in the past. Which didn't seem to be the case here. Unless…

Her gaze caught on the top of a large antique feed box in the corner, the lid askew.

"Oh, God, not the corn."

She kept her organic corn seeds in that box. She saved those seeds carefully year after year, since they were hard to come by. She always made sure the lid was closed tight so the occasional mouse couldn't get in. That corn was one of her most prized possessions. If something ate that…

She hurried closer, even as she thought, *A wild animal couldn't have opened the lid.* But she didn't relax when she found the corn still in place. The lid had definitely been moved. The short hairs stood up at the back of her neck. A wild animal couldn't lift the lid like that, she thought again.

A wild animal couldn't have gotten in here in the first place. The door hadn't been locked, but she did keep it barred. She turned in a slow circle, searching for holes in the floor and wall, the roof. She saw no hole that could have been an entry.

She squatted to examine the scratched floorboards, patting the dogs when they immediately came to lick her face. "I don't like the look of this."

The scratch marks were short and perfectly straight, not like what an animal would make.

"Crowbar," she muttered, and Skipper gave a sharp bark, as if agreeing.

"Oh, yeah? Where were you when this was happening?"

But she knew the answer. The dogs had been out here, barking. She'd heard them in the night. And she'd ignored them, thinking nothing of it. They had plenty of wildlife around; the dogs were always barking at something or other.

She stood and grabbed a rusty old screwdriver from the windowsill, then pried one of the floorboards up, then another and another, until she had a gap wide enough for a good look. Nothing under there but a foot-deep gap to the ground, filled with spiderwebs, then packed dirt. She set the boards back into place and looked around, trying to see the place through fresh eyes.

"Why would anyone break into the shed? Nothing's missing." She definitely didn't keep anything valuable here.

Had a drifter come by looking for food? Someone who'd come over the border in the night, stopping here for shelter? Maybe they'd tried to hide under the floor, then thought better of it on account of the rattlers that loved places like that. There was nobody down there now. She didn't stick her head all the way down to look, but the dogs would have let her know.

She mulled over the odd business while filling two dozen boxes from her garden, then she drove into town for groceries and to drop off her freshly picked vegetables at the Italian restaurant, and the milk at the cheese shop.

Running a fully working ranch of this size was too big of a task for her alone, so she made money any way she could, with her cows and her organic garden, with boarding horses or whatever opportunities came her way.

"Thanks," Ellie, the cheese maker, said. "I made this just for you." She handed over an herbed roll of soft cheese, Logan's favorite. "A gift. How are things at the ranch?"

What was she going to say? *I'm a person of interest in smuggling?* She forced a smile. "Everything is great." Then she hurried out before Ellie could think of any more questions.

The new, shiny black tires on her pickup—courtesy of her credit card—drew her eye. She hated the thought of how long it was going to take to pay them off. Great, now she was adding credit-card debt to the bills, on top of the mortgage.

Then an uncomfortable thought struck her and she stopped midstride. Were her slashed tires and last night's intruder connected? Could Moses Mann be right and some idiot was trying to send her a message?

On an impulse, she swung by the sheriff's office to ask him about the weird shed business.

"I normally wouldn't think anything of it, but someone slashed my tires in the driveway a couple of days ago," she told Shane as they stood by the reception desk, the small office buzzing with activity around them. They'd had layoffs recently, so everybody who remained had to double up on work.

He looked more annoyed than interested, probably figured he had bigger problems. "Maybe them tires just deflated."

"They had holes."

The sheriff shrugged. "Could have run over some nails in the road without noticing." He shuffled through a handful of pink phone-message slips.

"Will you come out to check the shed?"

He glanced up. The all-business look on his face was normally reserved for strangers. They'd known each other all their lives, but his features didn't soften any as he asked, "Anything missing?"

"No."

"You see anyone hanging around your place?"

"No."

"I have two dozen cases that take priority." He turned his back on her and walked away, toward his office.

"I wouldn't worry about it too much," Margie May, the receptionist, said, the only person at the station to show

Molly any sympathy. "Probably some illegals passing through in the night."

She nodded. That happened on occasion. She wasn't scared of them. They never went up to the houses. They didn't want trouble. All they wanted was to get up north unseen. One might have gone into the shed looking for food or water. But why would any of those people slash her tires? That didn't make any sense.

Margie May looked after the sheriff. "He'll come around. He's embarrassed over your brother. They hung out at the bar on game nights. He's gotten some flak for not realizing that one of his buddies was a criminal."

Molly stiffened as cold disappointment spread through her. "Dylan was *not* a criminal. He was framed." His exoneration could not come fast enough.

Margie May didn't comment, just went back to her typing.

Molly strode out and headed off to the grocery store. Dylan so did not deserve the way people treated him.

Her brother had always been the only one she could truly count on. She wasn't going to let him down. She was going to clear his name if it was the last thing she did.

She hurried through grocery shopping then went to the post office next. Missy Nasher, who'd always taken special pleasure in spreading rumors about her, stood at the end of the line.

If Missy saw her from the corner of her eye, she didn't acknowledge her. Instead, she backed right into Molly and knocked the package from her hand.

"Oh," she said as she turned around. Not *sorry*. Then put her nose in the air as she turned her back again, as if Molly was beneath her notice.

Missy struck up a conversation with the old woman in

front of her about what a shame it was that the sheriff's department was getting cut when crime was so obviously rampant in town. A direct dig at Dylan, no doubt.

Molly gritted her teeth, keeping her mouth shut. When the paper printed an apology, Missy and the rest of them would stand corrected.

Whatever people say about others, it always tells more about them than the person they're speaking about. Wasn't that what she always told Logan?

"How are you doing, Molly? I'm really sorry about your brother."

She turned to the man behind her, feeling ridiculously grateful for the kind words. Her muscles relaxed a little as she smiled her gratitude at Kenny Davis, the Pebble Creek sheriff. "Thank you, Kenny."

Kenny had gone to high school with Dylan. Good to see that he, at least, wasn't turning his back on that friendship.

He gave her a warm smile. "How are things at the ranch?"

"All right." She didn't want to discuss her latest troubles with half a dozen people listening in.

"Old Woodward still renting?"

She didn't work the whole ranch, couldn't have handled it on her own. She had her gardens and a handful of animals. Most of her income came from what Henry Woodward paid her for renting her land as additional grazing ground for his steers. "He doesn't get out much anymore. His sons have taken over," she said.

"Any trouble with rustlers?"

"Not that I heard of." With the economy being what it was, rustling was coming back, like in the old days.

Missy gave two letters to the postmaster, paid and left with head held at a haughty angle.

Molly stepped up to the window at last and handed over her package, returning a pair of boots she'd ordered online that turned out to be too large.

She said goodbye to Kenny on her way out, but he caught up with her again in the parking lot. His police cruiser stood next to her old pickup.

"I was heading over to grab some coffee." He gestured with his head toward the diner across the road. "How about it? I have a horse that needs to be boarded. I hoped we might be able to talk about that."

She hesitated for a moment. *The diner.* Did she want to put herself through that? The speculative glances… If someone said something nasty about her brother, God help her—

Oh, to hell with it. She wasn't going to run and hide. She had a life in this town. She was going to raise her son here. She had just as much right to be at the diner as anybody else did, regardless of what they all erroneously thought about her brother.

Nobody would accost her with the sheriff by her side, would they?

She forced a smile onto her face. "That would be nice." And she kept that smile as they walked across the road together.

Kenny wasn't overly tall, just a few inches taller than she. In high school, he'd been quite the heartthrob. He'd paid no attention to her back then, of course. None of her brother's friends on the football team had. They had their eyes on the cheerleaders. She'd been just a scrawny kid to them.

Despite the years that had passed since, he was still handsome, more handsome in the traditional sense than Moses Mann. Two of Kenny could have fitted into Mo, who was built like a tank and had a nose that looked as if it had been the landing place for a number of well-aimed punches. And with that half-missing left eyebrow, Mo had some sort of warrior vibe that Kenny lacked. It probably drew women in droves. Not that she cared. She pushed the thought away. Why was she comparing the two men, anyway?

"Booth or table?" the waitress asked as soon as they walked through the door.

"Booth," Kenny responded.

Molly ignored the curious looks as they were seated.

"Pie?" Kenny pointed to the large color ad on the wall, pretty enough to set her mouth salivating. "The chocolate-meringue pie is killer here."

"Better stick with the coffee." On her short frame, any extra pounds showed way too fast. She'd gained several since Dylan's death. She needed to stop trying to eat her grief.

"So what was that in there with Missy Nasher?" Kenny asked with an easy smile.

Oh, God, he'd noticed that, had he?

She gave a dismissive shake of her head. "She never really liked me. It doesn't matter. Old high-school rivalry."

Kenny drew up an eyebrow. "People who stick their noses in the air like that usually fall flat on their faces sooner or later."

The support felt nice. "Thanks."

But the truth was, even beyond Missy, she'd never been one of the popular people in town. She had never told anyone who Logan's father's was, which had started a rumor that he was a married man. It made most married women hate her on sight, because they wondered if it was their husband she'd slept with. And of course, married men went out of their way to avoid her so as not to fall under the cloud of suspicion.

Some of the single guys had come around, thinking she was an easy conquest. When she turned them down, they got offended and spread false rumors to pay her back for the rejection.

"Hullett is a small town with small-town morals. People have little to do for entertainment but gossip about their neighbors," Kenny was saying. "Move to Pebble Creek."

"Because that's, what, five hundred heads bigger?" she teased.

"All right, then just ignore the idiots here."

Easier said than done. With Dylan's death, the gossip mill was running full force again. But she nodded.

"Must be difficult out there alone," he said after the waitress filled their mugs.

She took a sip, the coffee burning the tip of her tongue. She set the mug down. "I'll manage."

He shook his head. "Having to go through Dylan's things can't be easy."

She closed her eyes for a second. "I haven't done it yet."

He leaned forward in his seat. "If you need help—"

She shook her head. "Not ready for that yet. But thank you." She could handle only so much at once. Someday she would deal with all that, but for now she was still grieving.

"You ever think about selling?"

She forced a smile. "Are you buying?"

He gave a white-toothed smile. "I wish I had the money. It's a fine piece of land."

She nodded. The farm had been in her family for generations.

"I have the animals," she said. "And I like it there. It's

the only place I've ever lived." The only place her son had ever lived, too.

And it would stay that way if she got her wish. She wasn't exactly a big fan of change. Change always brought trouble.

Kenny stirred his coffee. "Still, out there, alone…"

"I have the dogs." Who weren't exactly guard dogs, admittedly. She took another sip, more carefully than the first time. Her ranch wasn't in Kenny's jurisdiction, but he was so nice to her, while Shane was such a… "I think someone's been in one of the outbuildings last night," she blurted.

Kenny sat up straighter, his full attention on her. "What happened? Did they take anything?"

"Nothing's missing. It's weird." She told him about the scratches on the floorboards and the rest. Then she told him about her tires.

"You should be careful. Illegal crossings have slowed to a trickle, with the economy as it is, but there's still smuggling. Those are not people you want to tangle with."

That he believed her and didn't brush her off like Shane felt nice. Kenny was a good guy. He'd always been a good friend to Dylan. "I'm always careful."

"Maybe you should move into Dylan's apartment in Hullett," he suggested. "I'd be happy to help you. In the meantime, I'll make sure to drive by the ranch when I'm on the night shift. It's not my jurisdiction, but—" He shrugged. "Helping friends is what it's about, right?"

Was he her friend? She felt grateful for the sentiment. She didn't have too many friends these days. So she nodded and thanked him, then asked about that horse that needed boarding. A little bit of extra money always came in handy. And even beyond that, she was happy to help Kenny out if she could.

Making a friend was exactly what she needed.

"If anything else happens, you come to me," he told her. "It might be even better not to involve Shane at all."

"He's just upset over Dylan."

Kenny shrugged. "If Dylan was framed, we have no way of knowing right now who framed him." He grimaced, as if having said more than he'd meant to say.

She leaned forward, her mind buzzing suddenly. "You mean Shane could be involved?" She had a hard time believing that. She'd known Shane forever.

Kenny made a dismissive gesture. "Maybe not Shane, but somebody from his office. A couple of times a year, we bust someone either on the police force or at CBP for selling out to the smugglers."

His face turned serious. "If you find out anything about Dylan and all the bad business that went down, you come to me. Promise me, Molly."

"I promise."

SINCE SHE WASN'T HOME, Mo walked around the house and the outbuildings. He wasn't sure if he was doing it to check that everything was okay and she was safe, or because he was trying to find evidence that she'd been in cahoots with her brother.

He didn't like the ambiguity. It hadn't happened to him often. He'd always been able to keep his professional and personal lives separate.

The dogs followed him around, tails wagging, tongues lolling, a goofy bunch. He sincerely hoped she wasn't counting on them for protection. He checked the outbuildings, since she kept them all unlocked. Everything looked fine. Until he stepped into the shed. He didn't like what he found there.

He had worked himself into a right dark mood by the time her red pickup rolled down the road and pulled into the driveway.

"Someone's been here, searching your place," he said in the way of greeting as he strode forward to meet her. "Any idea who that might have been?"

She stood by her vehicle, her posture stiff. "What are you doing here?"

The jean shorts and pink tank top she wore kicked his heart rate up a notch. "Checking on you."

He lusted after her body. So there, he admitted it. He appreciated her curves, her loyalty to her brother and her dedication to her son, and was drawn by that hint of vulnerability in her eyes. She wasn't tough the way Grace Cordero was or some of the women he'd worked with on overseas missions. Yet she was plenty strong in her own way. She intrigued him.

He pushed all that out of his mind. "Somebody was out here, looking for something."

"I know. Last night."

"Who?"

"Maybe someone headed north, looking for food."

"Under floorboards?"

She stayed silent.

"The same week that someone slashed your tires?" He shook his head. "Too much of a coincidence for my taste. It could be one of your brother's smuggling partners looking for something."

"My brother had no smuggling partners, because he wasn't smuggling anything. Just as nobody was trying to send me a message with those tires. This has nothing to do with Dylan." She emphasized the last words, saying them slowly, as if she thought he had trouble understanding.

Part of him wanted to let her have the fantasies that she clung to. But with the situation she was in, denial could be dangerous. He didn't want her in danger.

He looked her straight in the eye. "You need to accept the truth so you can start dealing with it."

She stuck out her chin, her spine ramrod straight. "If I want free life-management advice, I'll tune in to Dr. Phil. I do own a television," she said in an icy tone, instead of telling him to go to hell. Oh, but she wanted to. Her eyes flashed with fire.

She had plenty of restraint, but underneath all that she hid heat and passion. Not that he needed to be intrigued any further by Molly Rogers. He filled his lungs. He was here for a reason.

He cleared his throat. "Do you know a Garcia Cruz?"

Her eyes narrowed. "Who?"

"Have you ever heard the name before? Maybe from your brother?"

She shook her head. "Who is he?"

"Are you aware of any links between your brother and the local gangs?"

She rolled her eyes at him. "There are no gangs in Hullett."

He nearly rolled his eyes back at her. "How about we let go of the delusion that small towns are paradises untouched by crime and that bad things happen only in the inner cities?" She needed a reality check, and he was the man to give it to her. "Who do you think handles the drugs and the guns and all the other illegal activity?"

She stared at him.

Could she be that naive? Maybe she was, living out here in the middle of nowhere, her life revolving around the ranch and her son. But oblivious was a dangerous way to be in today's world.

He didn't like the thought of her out here alone with only an eight-year-old for company. "You should stay in town for a while in your brother's apartment."

"I have animals."

"You can drive out twice a day to do what needs to be done. You don't need to spend the nights out here."

"The apartment hasn't been released yet."

"Still?" That seemed odd. It had been searched, everything cataloged. It wasn't a crime scene. He wondered what the holdup was. "I'll see what I can do about that. I don't want you here alone at night."

"I don't want to move." She turned her back to him, signaling that was her final word on the subject, then went around to the passenger side of the pickup to grab some groceries. He helped her, even though it only earned him a glare.

"Where is Logan?" he asked.

"In school."

"Any more trouble?"

She shook her head.

"He must miss your brother."

She stared for a moment, then blinked hard. She turned away and began walking toward the house. "I don't think he can even fully comprehend that Dylan is gone forever. I'm not sure I can. Sometimes I still almost call him to check when he'll be home for dinner."

She wasn't one of those stick women a man was afraid to look at for fear of breaking, but there was an aura of fragility to her as she walked away from him, and he suddenly had to fight the urge to comfort her. "I'll stop by as often as I can."

"I'd prefer it if you didn't."

"It'd be good for whoever is messing with you to see that you're not alone."

"Nobody is messing with me," she said over her shoulder. "It's all just random stuff. Bored teenagers."

She was in denial through and through, about too many things. He wanted her to be careful, to be safe, but for that, she first had to admit that she was in danger.

So when they were inside and the grocery bags were sitting on the table, he reached for her and turned her to him before she could bustle away. His palms tingled on her bare skin. In addition to tingles in other places.

He let his hands fall. He seriously needed to get over whatever crazy attraction he felt for her. So he focused on the trouble she was in. "I'd appreciate it if you kept what I'm about to say between us. It's part of our investigation."

She stepped back from him but nodded.

"The same knife that was used to slash your tires was also used in a vicious gang murder. The people who are coming around here, they are the wrong kind of people, Molly."

Chapter Three

"Almost done," Molly said, patting Nelly's flank as she finished up the evening milking. The smell of hay and fresh milk filled the barn, but her thoughts were only partially on what she was doing. They kept returning to Moses Mann, as they had all through the day.

He had told her she should stay away from the ranch at night for a while. Kenny had said the same thing.

"I don't want to go anywhere," she told Nelly and the other cows.

But she wouldn't put her son in danger just because she wasn't good with change. So if things got worse… "I can do it if I have to."

Nelly's gaze was doubtful, but the other cows nodded in silent support as they chewed their cud.

The first step was to have the apartment released, then she would have an option, at least, whether or not she decided to take it. Grace could do it. She'd move anywhere in the blink of an eye. She'd traveled the world with the Army. If Grace could go someplace where people were shooting at her, Molly thought, then she could go to Hullett, for heaven's sake.

She set the milk pails out of kicking distance from Nelly, her most ornery cow, then pulled out her phone and called the police station again. Margie May answered.

"It's Molly. Is Shane in yet?"

"Just went out on another call."

"I would really like access to my brother's apartment. I need to know when I can come in to pick up the keys. Could you have him call me back?"

"Sure, hon."

"That's what you said before," she said without accusation. Shane was avoiding her, and they both knew it.

A moment of silence passed between them. "Listen. I think, and I shouldn't be telling you this…" Margie May paused. "Since Shane missed the whole thing that was going on with Dylan, he wants to score some points in the rest of the investigation. So he's going through everything with a fine-tooth comb. All the reports, the apartment, your brother's truck. It might be a while yet."

"He is doing all that?" Relief washed over her. "Thanks."

If Shane was giving the case his full attention, he would realize sooner or later that Dylan had been framed. She wanted that, first and foremost. Maybe an official announcement of Dylan's innocence would get whoever was harassing her to quit. If people thought Dylan had drugs and Lord knew what else stashed around the ranch…

Mo's ominous announcement about gang connections sent chills running down her spine every time she thought of it. The knife that had slashed her tires had been used in a murder. That was creepy and scary.

And it didn't make any sense whatsoever.

The gang murder had happened in San Antonio, according to Mo. She barely knew anyone in the city, certainly no criminals.

She grabbed the milk pails, said good-night to the cows and closed up the barn. Then she glanced at the light in Logan's window.

He'd already had his dinner and bath and was in bed,

playing "Calvin Cat Counting" on his handheld player. The game taught kids math without them realizing they were learning. Logan loved the action; she loved the A's he brought home.

Learning was a big thing in the house; she'd made sure of that. And so was eating healthy and running around outside in fresh air. She tried to make up for her son not having a father and was raising him to the best of her abilities.

She took the milk to the old farm kitchen at the back of the house where she processed everything she sold. A car came up the driveway as she reached the door. A police cruiser. Kenny. She stopped and waited for him.

The dogs ran to check him out then dashed back to her, not nearly as excited about the visitor as they usually were about Mo. As much as Mo annoyed her, her animals and Logan seemed to like him. Logan had asked if he could go on a ride in his fancy car with him. Probably just wanted to push the siren button.

Kenny waved at her then walked back to where she waited for him. "Thought I'd make sure everything is all right out here."

"Pretty good so far." Aside from Mo's startling revelation, which she couldn't talk about. "Are you bringing the horse this weekend?"

"Charlie. He's a good one. In a couple of days."

She walked into the processing room and he came in after her. The dogs stopped outside the door. They knew they weren't allowed in there. She didn't want dog hair in the milk she sold.

"Night shift?" she asked as she screened the milk through cheesecloth, making sure it didn't have any stray pieces of hay.

He shook his head. "Just coming off shift. Long day.

Had a couple of speed traps up today. Weekend comes and people start driving like they're on a racetrack."

"Hand out any tickets?"

He gave a smug smile. "Filled up the tiller."

She tidied up. "I better close up for the night."

He followed her out and took his time looking around the shed, but said nothing about the break-in, just shook his head. She was tempted to ask his advice on the gang angle, the words on her lips a couple of times, but each time she held back, as Mo had asked.

The chickens were in their coop already, had gone in on their own once it started getting dark. All her animals knew the schedule. All she had to do was bar the doors so no stray coyote could get in. "You think I should put up padlocks?"

He thought about that for a second or two before he nodded. "I have a few extras at home. I can bring those over when I bring Charlie."

"Thanks."

"So coffee was nice the other day," Kenny said when they were finished. "How about we do it again? I would like to take you to dinner."

A second passed before full comprehension came. *A date.*

Wow. Okay.

She shifted from one foot to the other. It had been a while since she'd been asked out.

Kenny was…nice. She didn't feel any sparks, but so what? Her grandmother had always told her love grew with time. It started with respect. And she did respect Kenny. He was here trying to help, while most people would rather gossip about her and her brother.

She didn't want to offend him or alienate him. If she alienated any more people in her life, she'd have nobody left.

"Okay. Sure."

A confident smile spread across his face, as if he'd fully expected that answer. And why wouldn't he? He was a pretty good catch, young with a steady job and good looks, a good standing in the community.

"Tomorrow night?" he suggested.

"How about tomorrow afternoon? Maybe four-ish? Logan will be at the annual library treasure hunt from four to six." She could drop her son off, then pick him up later, have dinner in between.

"I'll come out to get you."

"I'll be in town anyway. Let's meet at the restaurant."

"I was thinking Gordie's?"

Gordie's served Tex-Mex cuisine, a nice place, but not so fancy that she would be uncomfortable. She nodded, trying not to think how fast they would set all the gossiping tongues wagging.

"Have a good night, then. See you tomorrow." Kenny flashed her another smile before he walked back to his car.

She looked after him as his dust-covered police cruiser pulled down the driveway.

Skipper came to lick her hand.

"I'm dating again. Okay, one date, but still, how weird is that?" she asked her, but if the dog thought it was weird, she kept it to herself. She just gave a goofy, lolling grin.

"I'm dating the Pebble Creek sheriff," Molly said experimentally. Yep, definitely sounded weird.

She went inside the house, letting the dogs in, picked up her yellow notepad from the windowsill where she'd left it earlier, and took it upstairs with her. She was working on a list of people she could ask for character references about Dylan, to submit to Shane. She wanted Shane to move the investigation in a new direction, help her figure out why and how her brother had been framed.

Maybe Kenny would help her.

She wished she was on speaking terms with Grace so she could call her friend and tell her all about that development. She hated the rift between them. But if she was against Dylan... No matter how good friends they'd been once, family came first.

At least Kenny was on her side.

As she got ready for bed, she tried to think of all the things she knew about him. He'd been one of the jocks back in high school, like her brother. Now he was a decent sheriff with a good record. He supported all kinds of fundraisers, was behind the department getting new cruisers a few years back. His department in Pebble Creek wasn't laying off like Shane's here in Hullett.

She wondered what Logan would think of him.

But even as she thought about Kenny while falling asleep, her dreams were filled with Moses Mann. Oddly, in her dreams, he didn't come to accuse or frame her. He came to protect her.

ANOTHER DAY, another interrogation room. This one, at the Hullett jail, was bigger than the one at the office trailer Mo's team used, but the furnishings were older and pretty banged up. Obviously, the place had seen a lot of use over the years.

Mo rolled his shoulders. He missed Molly Rogers. How stupid was that? He looked across the desk at Mikey Metzner, owner of the Hullett Wire Mill, Dylan Rogers's partner in crime in human trafficking. He was in his early thirties, a trust-fund yuppie who'd inherited his father's business. Obviously, he hadn't been satisfied with all that easy money. Maybe he was an adrenaline junkie.

He looked pretty confident still, after nearly a week behind bars, two fancy Dallas lawyers flanking him. He'd been questioned before and denied everything. He held the firm belief that his money was going to save him.

Mo was here to convince him of the error of his thinking.

"How long have you been in the smuggling business, Mr. Metzner?" He didn't mince words. He wasn't in the best of moods. He hated starting his Sunday morning by having to talk to jackasses like the one before him.

"You don't have to answer that," one of the lawyers said.

"I had no idea something so atrocious was going on at my mill. I'm as shocked as you are," Metzner said straight-faced, wearing his best pious expression. "I can't tell you how terrible I feel that somebody would use my mill for something so completely reprehensible."

Give the man a golden statue, Mo thought morosely as he leaned forward in his seat. "Your hired men are out-doing each other confessing, blaming everything on you, hoping for a plea bargain."

Unfortunately, they had nothing valuable. The handful of underlings his team had caught only knew their own tasks.

He fixed Mikey with a flat look. "Who else was involved in running things on this side of the border beyond you and Dylan Rogers?"

"I have no idea what you're talking about."

"We have multiple, signed confessions from your goons, naming you the head of the operation in Hullett. Do you really want to take the rap for this?"

"I was head of nothing." The man's shoulders stiffened as he looked from one lawyer to the other, then back at Mo. "You can't believe anything those people say. They are the ones responsible. I'll testify against them."

Mo shrugged. "We already have all we need for a conviction. We caught them red-handed."

The bastard's face paled. Cold sweat broke out on his forehead. "What do you want from me?"

"A name. Who is the third partner?"

One of the lawyers coughed.

Mikey straightened and started talking stiffly, as if repeating a prerecorded message. "I wasn't involved in any smuggling. Whatever was going on in the basement at the mill, it had nothing to do with me. I'm a respectable businessman. I provide several hundred jobs in this community. The public is not going to be happy if those jobs disappear."

Mo shrugged again. "Public patience is running out with all the dirty dealings on the border. Local elections are coming up. Results need to be demonstrated. Somebody is going to be made an example of. The higher up in the chain of command in the smuggling ring, the better. So far, you're the highest we have."

He ignored the lawyers and pinned Metzner with a hard look. "Multiple counts of kidnapping, moving persons across international borders, child exploitation, human trafficking." He paused. "I could go on, but I'm in a hurry."

He pushed his chair back and stood. "Better get used to the idea of a maximum sentence. I have two words for you, Mikey—federal prison."

Metzner's Adam's apple bobbed. "There's no way I'm going to prison. You can't scare me. This is police intimidation. This is harassment."

Mo held the man's gaze. "You want harassment, wait till you're behind bars. You've gone soft from office work, Mikey. Life in prison's not gonna be pretty."

The man stared at him, radiating hate. A few seconds of silence passed before he said, "Look, I was brought in because I had the mill and it has a lot of room. Nobody notices a couple of extra Mexicans coming and going. None of this was my idea."

"Yeah, sure. Practically a victim," Mo said dispassionately. He didn't move toward the door, but neither did he sit back down. "Give me a name."

"I don't know anything."

"Give me a name."

"Look." His head snapped up. "I know Dylan was working with someone in town, but I don't know who. My only contact was Dylan. I swear."

Threatening him hadn't worked before, and it didn't look as if it would work now. He was too full of himself to truly believe he couldn't beat the charges.

Which gave Mo an idea. Maybe playing on the man's ego would work better.

"I understand. They didn't trust you. They didn't think you could handle it. They played you because they figured you weren't smart enough to know that you were being played."

"I'm plenty smart. Smarter than them."

"How do you figure?"

"Dylan is dead and I'm alive," he said, smug-faced.

"Yet you have nothing to give me to make your life easier."

Metzner rubbed his fingertips together. "If you drop the charges…"

Mo watched him carefully. So there *was* something. "Not going to happen. You tell me what you have, and it'll be taken into consideration at your sentencing."

Metzner looked at his lawyers. They were scowling, but the older one nodded again.

"Coyote," Metzner said in a low tone. "I overheard Dylan a few months ago talking on the phone to someone. He was saying something about the Coyote being pissed because too many of his mules were getting busted lately."

Now they were getting somewhere. He grabbed the back

of his chair and leaned on it. "You think this Coyote was Dylan's other friend who handles the smuggling around here?"

Mikey shook his head. "Coyote is the one who's sending the mules."

The big boss on the other side of the border? Hell, if they could identify him, it would be the biggest break they'd caught so far.

But no matter how many questions Mo asked after that, that single name was the only thing Metzner could give him. He headed back into the office more frustrated than when he'd left it earlier that morning.

He was beginning to hate this op. When they were sent in for an overseas mission, there was usually a clear-cut enemy. They were generally in some jungle or on some Afghan mountainside, or in the desert where they could maneuver without fear of civilian casualties. They did rescues, assassinations or intelligence gathering.

Now they were in small-town America, pussyfooting around fellow citizens who were too stupid to realize that by violating the border, they were weakening national security. He was a low-key guy. He had a pretty good rein on his temper for the most. But he seriously wanted to beat Mikey Metzner's head into the damned desk back there. He couldn't stand it when someone was messing with his country.

"Anything?" Ray, a big chunk of Viking wearing a leg cast, asked as soon as Mo walked through the door. He and Jamie were working from the office that morning, comparing satellite images and analyzing CBP data, looking for likely crossing points across the Rio Grande.

The team had already discovered two tunnels. Both discoveries had been compromised, unfortunately. One of the tunnels had blown up, injuring Ray. The transfer would happen someplace else. The key was to find out where and let no one know that they knew the location. They wanted the transfer to go ahead as planned so they could apprehend those terrorists and their weapons.

"Not much," he answered Ray. "Yet. But we'll get them."

"We're gonna kick terrorist ass." Ray grinned. "That's what we do."

The sooner, the better. "This small-town business is more like detective work," Mo grumbled. "Having to treat dirtbags like Metzner with kid gloves while the tangos are getting a step closer to crossing the border rubs me the wrong way."

He'd been made for action, not for investigative detail.

"Prepare for more of this when you transfer to the CIA," Jamie put in. "It's not all fancy gadgets and pretty women like in the movies."

He knew that. He wanted it anyway. His foster father, the man who'd pretty much saved his life, had tried out for the agency. He didn't pass the test because of an old war injury from his Marine days. But it had been his dream. He had been through some bad breaks, had lost close friends in his platoon due to bad intelligence. He'd wanted to do something about that, bring combat experience to the agency.

He had tried to direct his sons that way, too, but none of them had an interest in the military, let alone intelligence services. Except Mo. He wanted to make the man proud, wanted to make that dream come true. It was such a small thing compared to what his foster father had done for him.

"Anyway, I did get one thing from Metzner," Mo said as he headed for the coffee. "A nickname. Coyote."

Ray swore. "Could be anyone."

"Guy is smart. You have to be to run a billion-dollar business. Still," Jamie said. "It's something we didn't have before. Could be a starting point. We can ask around."

Shep strode in just then, coming off border patrol.

"Anything?" Mo asked, hoping his teammate had better luck this morning.

"Interviewed a dozen ranchers near the border, border agents, even bird watchers." He shrugged. "Everybody says the same thing. Barely anyone is crossing these days. They think it's because of the economy."

"Or because the bastard in charge is having everyone lie low while he gets ready for his big move," Mo thought out loud.

Jamie pushed to his feet. "I better head out. All we need is one lucky break, catching one guy who knows something."

He had been hired as operations coordinator. Technically, he didn't have to leave the office. But he'd insisted on being put on the rotation, even though walking around with his prosthetic legs had to be exhausting, possibly painful. He never used that as an excuse. If anything, he pushed himself harder than anyone else. If Mo knew one thing, it was this: when they all fell down, Jamie Cassidy would still be standing.

He had the hardest eyes Mo had ever seen and very few emotions. He had a legendary record within the SDDU, not that he ever talked about past missions. Especially not about the one that had taken his legs. And everybody respected that.

"Mo got a name from Mikey Metzner," he told Shep. "Coyote."

"Sounds like it could be a gang name," Shep said as he dropped into his chair and turned on his computer.

"Makes sense. The man could have started out in the gangs then risen in the ranks." The gangs were connected to the smuggling, the smuggling was connected to Dylan Rogers, and Dylan Rogers was connected to whoever the third man was that controlled illegal activity in this specific area. The very man they needed. Even if he didn't know the Coyote's true identity, he would know how to get in touch with him.

Mo thought about that for another minute before his thoughts switched to something else. "Did you go by the Rogers Ranch on your way in?"

"Yeah," Shep said. "Just the red pickup in the driveway."

"Had a police cruiser out last night. The sheriff from Pebble Creek. Forgot to tell you," Ray added.

Kenny Davis, Mo recalled. He pushed to his feet. "What time?"

"Around eight."

He didn't like it. Molly hadn't called for help. They monitored the emergency services channels. "Wonder what he wanted."

Jamie shrugged. "Maybe he's investigating her brother's dealings, too."

Mo frowned. "It's not his jurisdiction."

Keith was watching him closely. "You seem very interested in this woman."

Mo put on his best poker face. "She's closely tied to the smuggling. Her brother played an integral part."

"So you think she's involved?"

"No," he admitted after a long second.

Ray raised an eyebrow and grinned. "She's pretty. Fine curves."

Mo shot the big Viking a look. "She's got a kid."

"So?"

"Keep your dirty eyes off her."

Ray laughed out loud. "It's like that, huh?"

Now Jamie, too, was grinning.

"It's not like anything." He just didn't want any harm

to come to her or Logan. The idea of those two in danger because of her idiot brother bothered him.

"Hey," Ray said to Jamie. "If Molly Rogers and Mo hooked up, would their celebrity nickname be Mo-Mo?"

Jamie gave a bark of a laugh. "How about just Moo?"

Mo stepped forward. "How about I knock your heads together?" he offered without heat. They ribbed each other all the time, pretty much part of the op. It allowed for letting off some steam.

Ray lifted his hands in a defensive gesture. "Listen, we're nothing if not supportive."

Jamie's grin widened.

Mo gave them a disgusted look, made sure he had his gun and his wallet, and headed for the door. "I'm heading into Hullett. Want to look at Dylan Rogers's apartment again." Wanted to talk to the Hullett sheriff about that, too. Why the place hadn't been released to Molly yet. Maybe the sheriff had found something he wasn't sharing.

He was at his car when his cell phone rang. Keith, the youngest guy on the team, was calling in. He'd been gathering intelligence on the other side of the border. The gun, drug and human smuggling in the area all seemed to be connected.

"Picking up bits and pieces of clues here and there. Not nearly enough." Frustration laced Keith's voice. "The human trafficking was set up for Hullett, with the help of the wire mill. But so far everything I have says the drugs are coming through Pebble Creek and distributed from there. I think different crews are running those two businesses."

"Makes sense. If one is busted, the other is still running. Probably a third crew runs the guns. Anyone mention the name Coyote?"

"No. Who is he?"

"Might be the big boss on that side."

"I'll see what I can find out."

They talked for another minute before hanging up. Mo drove by the Rogers ranch on his way to town. Nothing suspicious out there. The driveway stood empty.

Since it was nearly four o'clock by the time he reached Hullett and he hadn't had lunch yet, he drove down Main Street, considering popping into the diner and grabbing a quick meal. But as he parked, he spotted Molly going into Gordie's across the street.

Wearing a pretty blue summer dress.

Two young guys turned after her, checking her out, but she was oblivious to her admirers, just smoothed her dress down and walked inside, looking a little nervous.

Mo crossed the road and went in after her. Might as well ask her if she had any trouble last night, why the Pebble Creek sheriff was over at her place. He wanted to make sure she was okay. But as he stepped into the restaurant, he spotted the man in question getting up from a table in the back and greeting Molly with a big smile.

For a moment, Mo stood and stared.

They're on a damned date.

Man, he felt stupid. And then he knew at once what Kenny had been doing at her place last night.

His jaw clenched, even as a perky blonde waitress hurried over to him.

She flashed a toothy smile. "How many are in your party?"

"I was just looking for someone. Thanks. They're not here." He turned on his heel and stalked out. The sight of the sheriff with Molly twisted his insides as if he'd swallowed poison. What the hell was wrong with him?

SAYING YES TO KENNY had been a mistake. She knew it five minutes into dinner, but at that point, it would have been

inexcusably rude to get up and walk away. She appreciated all Kenny was doing for her, but whatever her grandmother had said about love growing over time, she knew
at a gut level that nothing whatsoever was ever going to
grow between them. Even the least spark of chemistry was
completely missing.

She had more chemistry with Moses Mann, for heaven's
sake, and that man thought she was a criminal.

"I can probably find a buyer for Dylan's truck," Kenny
was saying as they walked out of the restaurant after dinner. They'd talked more about her brother than anything
else. "After the police release it."

"That would be great." Whatever money she got for
that she would immediately put into the new mortgage on
the ranch.

A pink convertible pulled up in front of the diner next
to them. Four women about her age got out, laughing and
teasing each other. They had matching tattoos on their
shoulders, maybe some sort of a sorority symbol. They
joked about their cross-country drive that sounded like a
grand adventure.

They looked wild and free, and she felt a sudden pang
of envy. She'd done everything possible in the past eight
years not to raise any eyebrows, to become a respectable
mother, someone people didn't whisper about. She didn't
want Logan to have to struggle with that in school like she
had to with her mother's reputation back in the day.

Her wild side scared her. She'd given in to it once and
ended up with the wrong man. She'd had to pay for that
every day since. She'd learned her lesson. Safe was always best.

Kenny looked safe enough. He was a sheriff.

Why couldn't she feel some attraction toward him?

He was looking her over, his interest clear in his gaze. "Wish I could drive you home."

She was flattered. She really was. But she wasn't interested.

"Got the pickup right here." She stepped toward her car. "Have to go get Logan from the library."

Kenny leaned forward, probably to kiss her on the cheek. She headed him off by lifting her hand for a quick wave and stepping back at the same time. Then she turned to search for her car keys in her purse. She didn't look up until she found them.

"Thank you for dinner. It was really nice to catch up." Was it too late to start pretending that the past hour and a half had been just a friendly meeting?

Kenny watched her for a second. "I'll see you around, then. I have the night shift tonight. I'll be driving by to make sure everything is all right out your way."

"Thanks," she said sincerely. Kenny wouldn't work as a boyfriend, but she was more than grateful to have him as a friend. Maybe she could pay him back in some small measure with a basket of goodies from her garden. And by taking extra-special care of his horse. Not that she didn't pretty much spoil all her animals rotten.

She drove over to the library, wishing once again that she had Grace to discuss her date with. Maybe Grace would talk her into trying harder. Heaven knew she was pitifully lonely these days. Somebody to share her life with would be nice.

She kept thinking about that as she drove to pick up her son, not liking at all that for some reason Moses Mann kept popping into her head.

"Look what I won, Mom!" Dylan held up a bag of books, his face radiating joy.

"I'm so proud of you. How about I take you for ice cream?"

"Ice cream!" He was hopping on one foot in excitement all the way to the car, then chatted on the drive to the ice-cream shop, filling her in on everything that had happened at the treasure hunt.

All right, so a boyfriend would have been nice, she thought, but as long as she had Logan, she was more than okay. The most important thing was that her son was happy.

They had ice cream, drove home singing to country songs on the radio, did their evening chores. After dinner, they moved on to their bedtime routine. Then she did some more work, washing glass jars, getting ready for the last of the canning. Eleven o'clock rolled by before she fell into bed, exhausted. But her rest was short-lived.

Shortly after midnight, she woke to the dogs barking outside.

Probably a coyote, she thought, fuzzy-brained. She turned onto her other side and tried to go back to sleep, but the dogs wouldn't give up. Then she came awake enough to remember the shed and all her recent problems with people prowling her property. Her heart rate picked up as she slipped from the bed.

She left the lights off so she could look outside and not be seen. Plenty of moonlight filtered into the room to make sure that she wouldn't trip on anything, so she shuffled to the nearest window.

The door on one of the outbuildings hung open. Had she forgotten to close the latch? No, she couldn't have. She'd been paying extra attention to make sure everything was closed up tight.

She tried to see the dogs but couldn't. One of them cried out, the long whine cutting through the night. She hurried downstairs and jumped into her boots. Then she stopped in her tracks when she thought about Mo's revelation that the knife used to slash her tires had also been used in a murder.

The dog whined again. She wasn't going to hide in here while one of her animals suffered, dammit. Who knew if Mo was even telling the truth? Could be he was just trying to scare her into spilling her brother's supposed secrets. She grabbed one of Dylan's rifles to be on the safe side and reached for the door, but then froze in her tracks as she put her hand on the doorknob.

She could see through the glass as a shadow, a human shadow, slipped from the outbuilding and ran around it, the dogs in close pursuit.

She opened the door and whistled for the dogs.

She had to whistle repeatedly before they came at last. She ordered them inside then locked the door and the doggie door. Then she went around to make sure all the other doors and windows were locked tight, too. And then she dialed Kenny. Shane and the Hullett police couldn't care less about her.

The phone rang and rang, but Kenny didn't pick up.

Her gaze fell on the card Mo left on her fridge. Okay, so it was possible he'd been right. Maybe someone *was* out there trying to do her harm.

Mo refused to believe that Dylan was innocent, but at least he cared about her and her son's safety. She dialed his number.

He picked up on the first ring. "Are you okay?" he asked before she could even say her name.

She had to raise her voice to be heard over the barking dogs that were jumping on the door, wanting to be let out. "There's someone outside."

"Go upstairs." His voice snapped tight. "Barricade yourself in one of the bedrooms with Logan and the dogs. I'll be right there. You have a gun with you?"

"Yes."

"If you need to use it, use it," he said before he hung up.

She had to practically drag the dogs upstairs with her. They wanted to go back outside, barking their heads off.

Waking up Logan, too.

"What happened, Mom?" he asked, sleepy-eyed, as she dragged the dogs into his room and locked the door behind them.

"Probably an armadillo."

His eyes closed. Then opened again. "Can I have pancakes for breakfast?"

"Sure. But it's not morning yet. You go back to sleep."

He drifted off again as the dogs jumped onto the bed and settled down around him in a protective circle.

An eternity passed before she heard a car pulling up her driveway. Which set the dogs barking again. She was pretty sure it was Mo, but since she couldn't see the front from Logan's room, she stayed put, hanging on to the gun.

Whoever it was didn't try to come into the house. But soon she did see Mo going around back, walking from outbuilding to outbuilding, checking everything. For the first time, she found his bulk and the determined way he moved reassuring. And she relaxed. Which was so stupid. She shouldn't relax around Mo. His presence shouldn't make her feel safe.

He wanted to pin multiple murders on her brother. He was scarcely her friend. And yet, she did feel better for having him here.

He spent half an hour doing a thorough job of checking every building before he came to the back door and knocked. "It's me."

"Coming." She padded downstairs to let him in. The dogs saw their chance and rushed out as soon as the door opened, this time ignoring her calls to get back inside.

He pretty much filled the doorway as he stood on the threshold, looking her over. "Are you and Logan okay?"

And there came that sense of safety again. As if everything was fine now just because he was here. She wanted to throw herself into his arms in relief. Which was an impulse beyond crazy, and very distracting.

He had to repeat his question before it finally reached her brain and she nodded.

"Did you see who it was?"

"Just a shadow."

"One person or more?"

"I only saw one." She reached for the kitchen light.

He put his large hand over hers. "In case somebody is out there still, let's not give them a target."

"You looked."

"Around the buildings. You can pick someone off with a good rifle from a fair distance."

Her stomach tightened at the thought. "Why would anyone want to hurt me?"

He seemed distracted. Kind of staring at her. And as she looked down, she realized she was standing in a shaft of moonlight, wearing nothing but her skimpy summer nightgown.

"Molly." His voice was low and thick.

Her gaze flew up and met his, and she found his eyes filled with hunger.

Tension ratcheted up and up between them. And then heat. All the heat that she'd been missing with Kenny.

Chapter Four

He'd been doing commando work long enough to have a sixth sense for knowing when trouble was coming.

Molly Rogers was trouble.

And the need that pulsed through his body as he took in her curves in the lavender silk gown was the least of it.

She stepped around him to the peg board by the back door, grabbed a summer cardigan and wrapped it around herself. He only registered disappointment where he should have felt relief. He didn't need the distraction.

He liked too many things about her. Her loyalty to her brother. Her devotion to her son. That she dealt with whatever came her way, worked the ranch, took care of everything with dignity and without complaint.

He'd asked around town about her. Found the town gossip at the diner. Mrs. Martin had called Molly "loose," not the kind of woman a decent man would get tangled with. But when Mo went after specifics…

"So she's in town and in and out of bars every night?" he'd asked.

"Well, no. She doesn't really do bars," the woman admitted with some reluctance.

"With a different man, then, every week, flaunting her boyfriends around town?"

"Not like that."

"Men go visit her at the ranch?"

"Probably. Just like her mother. It's in the blood. Women like her draw men to sin."

Okay, that he could picture. She certainly inspired sinful thoughts in him.

"You know any of the men?"

"She was here with a *sheriff* the other day. And I'm sure there are many others." Then came a meaningful look. "She never told anyone who her son's father is, you know. There has to be a reason for *that*."

At the end, he found out nothing new about Molly, but had felt dirtier for the gossip.

He had no trouble talking to her in the interrogation room, but he had no idea what to tell her now, in the middle of the night in her dark kitchen, with her standing there semi-naked. He wasn't exactly a ladies' man like some of the guys on his team.

He wanted her. He couldn't tell her that. For one, he had no business wanting her. He was here on an op, an op that was tied to her brother, even if she *was* innocent like he was believing more and more with every passing day.

"I hope Logan didn't get scared," he said. There, her son should be a safe subject.

She looked toward the stairs. "Barely woke up. Went right back to sleep." She turned from him and walked to the fridge. "I'm sorry for bothering you in the middle of the night. Thank you for coming out. Would you like a cold drink?"

"No bother. And a drink would be great."

She poured him sweet tea. "Sun-made." She filled a glass for herself then sat at the kitchen table by the window and looked out.

He followed her gaze to keep his eyes from sliding to

her bare legs. On second thought… He sat across the table from her. Better have something tangible between them.

Moonlight bathed the outbuildings in a silver glow, the stars bright in the sky. With very little pollution out here in the country, every star in the whole universe seemed visible from where they were sitting.

He liked sitting with her in the night, drinking her sweet tea and looking at the stars. He liked it too much. Being with her somehow made him feel as if he'd been lonely all his life, until now. Which was ridiculous. With back-to-back ops, he'd never had time to be lonely.

He shifted in his seat and tried to focus on things he should be focusing on. "Anything you can tell me about your brother will only help."

She drew back, her face hardening in a split second. A different kind of tension filled the air. "Who would it help? Not him. He's dead. Killed by one of the men you work with."

"If we had some answers, it would help you and Logan. Too many things are going on at the ranch. All the smuggling we discovered so far is not a good thing. And it might be just the tip of the iceberg." That was as much as he could tell her.

"Dylan was not a smuggler."

"You're not going to be able to move on until you face the truth. And you're not going to be safe until we figure out who his partners were and what exactly they were doing with him. They clearly want something from you. Your best chance at staying safe is if you help me take these men out of circulation."

Her lips flattened. "The truth is, my brother was framed. And the ranch is perfectly safe. The man…was probably just some drifter. It happens."

He looked at her for a long time. "You're a smart woman.

You've faced hardship before, but you made it work. You're raising your son just fine. You're handling the ranch…"

She cut him off. "I'm not in denial, if that's what you're getting at."

"Dylan—"

"Dylan can't be the bad guy." She shook her head stubbornly. "You don't understand. Dylan was always the perfect child in the family, the small-town football hero, then the successful businessman. I am the family goof-up."

She had plenty of conviction in her voice to tell him she fully believed that. Apparently, she saw herself in a completely different light than he saw her.

"I get it. Your brother was a very important part of your life. When people who are supposed to care about us do bad things, it's not an easy thing to face."

She shot to her feet, her hand grasping the back of her chair. "What would you know about that? I'm sure you grew up in a perfect family. I'm sure your father never drank, your mother never ran off with a stranger, you never had to—" She bit her lower lip.

A long moment of silence stretched between them.

"You think I have the perfect life?" He laughed out loud at that.

But she wouldn't give up. "You're strong. Whatever happens, you can defend yourself. You have all kinds of power, working for whoever you're working for. You're not at the mercy of anyone or anything. You have everything together."

He watched her. "And you?"

She let go of her chair and wrapped her arms around herself. "I have nothing together. I just lost my brother. People think he was a criminal. My son is getting into fights defending him. I can barely pay my bills. And strangers are coming to the ranch in the middle of the night for God knows what reason."

She sank back into her seat. "I'm a single mother. Half the time, I'm petrified of doing something wrong, not being able to protect my son, people being mean to him because of my mistakes." She shook her head. "I have nothing together. I'm just pretending that I do for Logan's sake."

They sat in the quiet of the night for a while after the confession ended, her gaze on the table. She was probably embarrassed that she'd told him all that.

He wished he knew what to say.

In combat, he was a well-trained fighting machine and pretty damned effective. With women, he was a bumbling idiot through and through. But she was in distress, and he hated the thought of that, wanted to say something to make it better if he could. He went with the stark truth, something he rarely, if ever, shared.

He stretched his legs out in front of him. "When I was born, my parents put me into a gym bag and dropped me into the Mississippi River from a bridge."

Her head snapped up. She stared at him. "I'm so sorry."

"Nothing to be sorry about. A Good Samaritan saw and fished me out. I went to foster care. Eventually ended up with the best family anyone could have wished for. Marine sergeant father, four older brothers, a mom who was kind and loving. They made me what I am today."

She sat silently for a long time. "What happened to your birth parents? It's just… It's unimaginable."

"It's unimaginable to you because you're a good mother. They were never identified."

"Are you still close to your foster family?"

"My mother and my father are gone. I keep in touch with my brothers." He didn't like the pity that sat on her face. "You might know one of them, actually. He's Calvin in 'Calvin Cat Counting.'"

"What?" Her eyes went wide. "Logan plays that game. Your brother is Calvin Mann? The guy who built an empire in educational software?"

"It's not that big of a deal. It's just a company."

Her eyes went wide. "Oh, my God. You're Mo."

He grinned. "I hope so. Otherwise, I'll have to have all new business cards printed."

"I mean, you're Mo the teddy bear, Calvin's best friend in the game."

He shook his head. "He did that without consulting me."

"Wait till Logan finds out." She laughed.

He couldn't help staring. She was pretty even under the worst circumstances, but when she laughed, she was dazzling. She should always be like that, happy and carefree.

But even as he thought that, she grew serious again. "Your name, Moses. Is it because…"

"Because I was pulled from water. The social worker who named me was a churchgoing woman." He finished his drink.

Molly watched him quietly, folding her hands together on the table in front of her. She opened her mouth, then closed it again. Then she finally said, "I want to tell you something, but I don't want you to make a big deal out of it."

His instincts prickled. She had his full attention. "Okay."

"Dylan took out a mortgage on the ranch," she said after a long minute. Then quickly added, "It doesn't mean he's a criminal. He could have needed the money for one of his businesses."

He chewed on the new piece of information for a few seconds. "Were you aware that he was having financial difficulties?"

She shook her head. "Maybe he wanted to expand the dealership."

"But he didn't say anything to you about it?"

"He had so many things going on. He was always running around. Sometimes he didn't even have time to stop in for dinner." She watched him. "Is there anything I could say to convince you that he was a good man?"

Moonlight glinted off her soft hair, for once loose and not up in a ponytail, the silky strands spilling over her shoulders. The silver light accentuated the wistful expression on her face. Every cell in his body responded to her. He didn't want to hurt her, but as far as her brother went...

"I believe he was good to you and Logan." He wanted to go around the table and pull her into his arms, offer her comfort he had no right offering. He pushed to his feet. "You get some sleep. I'm going back outside to check around again, walk in a wider circle."

She stiffened as she glanced to the window. "You think that man is still here?"

"It never hurts to be cautious. When the sun comes up, I'll find his tracks and take some tire molds. Maybe we can identify his vehicle."

She walked him to the door.

He stepped outside into the night. "Lock it behind me."

She looked worried. The urge to touch her, to smooth the furrows from her forehead, came on pretty strong. He wished he were more comfortable with women, more of a charmer, someone who could make a woman like her look differently at him.

But he wasn't. And she was dating the Pebble Creek sheriff.

So he walked away.

AFTER MOLLY PUT LOGAN on the school bus Monday morning, she paid her bills online, then looked Moses Mann up on Google while she had her second cup of coffee. Max and Cocoa were somewhere outside. Only Skipper lazed around in the kitchen, lying on the doormat by the back door. The old gal probably tuckered herself out running around outside half the night.

Molly scrolled down the list of hits, a very short list. The few things she found, articles in various newspapers, were mostly about Mo's brother Calvin Mann. Mo only got a sentence or two, about his role in his brother's business. He was a silent partner, according to one report.

Apparently, he'd been on active duty with the military when Calvin had started the software company in the family basement. Mo had fronted the money for the entire operation from his combat pay.

The "Calvin Cat Counting" game was a huge hit among elementary-school-age children, one of the top-rated educational games in the country. And they followed up with dozens of others from K–12 education to SAT- and college-prep software. Which meant both Mo and his brother had to be multimillionaires.

So why wasn't he sitting on some tropical island, sipping margaritas?

Even as the question popped into her head, it made her smile. She couldn't really imagine Mo as a surfer dude. Granted, he could be laid-back, but…there was also an intensity inside him, a drive. For a moment she couldn't pin it down, and then she did: he had a soldier's heart.

He would spend all day in over hundred-degree heat patrolling the border. He would rush to her house in the middle of the night when she was in trouble.

He would make a fierce enemy—she wasn't going to forget that interrogation anytime soon. But she had a feeling he also made the most loyal friend.

What kind of lover would he make?

She squeezed her eyes shut. She couldn't believe she'd just thought that.

To distract herself, she went back to her computer search. He had no Twitter or Facebook accounts, no social-media presence of any kind.

Maybe because he worked for the government. He was a consultant on border protection. Did that require some kind of security clearance and secrecy? She had no idea about these things.

Skipper gave a pitiful moan.

"Tired?" She offered some sympathy as she shut down the laptop. "Me, too. Maybe we'll get a little more sleep tonight. Want to go for a walk? I need to check on the garden."

As she walked to the door, Skipper struggled to her feet, and once she stood, she swayed.

"What is it, girl? Is your back hurting again?"

The dog gave another pitiful whine and threw up all over the doormat.

She rushed to her, grabbing a roll of paper towels in the process. "What did you eat out there last night?"

Skipper was notorious for eating anything she came across. She'd once eaten half of a two-by-four in the garage before Molly had noticed. And a cell phone. Several shoes. A dead mouse from the mousetrap in the barn. With the trap. Food that was left out… Forget it. Although she did do her level best to keep anything remotely tempting out of the dog's way.

She cleaned up, gave the poor dog some cold water. "You'll feel better now that it's out. What do I always tell you about eating only what I put in your dish?" She ran her fingers through the dog's fur and scratched behind her ear.

She didn't like how Skipper's brown eyes were glazed over. Or the way her muscles suddenly began to shake.

"All right. We're going to the doc." She grabbed her purse and walked out, really worried now. "Come on."

Skipper staggered after her. She didn't make it to the pickup. For the last couple of yards, Molly had to carry her.

She called the other dogs and they came running. They seemed fine, no signs of any sickness. Didn't look as if they'd eaten whatever Skipper had.

"When you recover from this, you're going on a diet." She struggled to get the dog onto the passenger seat.

All Skipper did was give her a pitiful look and an even more pitiful whimper.

"You'll be fine, okay? Just relax. We'll fix this," she said once she was in the driver's seat. But her heart was racing.

Nothing could happen to Skipper. She'd been a graduation present from Dylan. She'd been with Molly most of her adult life. She was Logan's favorite, the most faithful dog in the universe.

She called the vet from the road, got the receptionist. "I'm bringing Skipper in."

"We have a substitute today. Won't be in until this afternoon. Dr. Miller is off."

"It's an emergency. Can I go out to his place?" She'd done that before. Dr. Miller didn't keep strict hours.

"He's at a conference in San Antonio. The sub will be in by noon."

Skipper couldn't wait a couple of hours. And Molly did know another vet, someone who had just recently passed her last exam and got her license.

Grace Cordero, her once best friend.

"I'll figure something out," she told the receptionist and hung up, then took the turn that would lead her to the Cordero ranch.

Whatever their differences were these days, she was

willing to set them aside when Skipper's life hung in the balance.

But would Grace? For some reason Grace thought Dylan had tried to hurt her. Cold panic tingled down Molly's spine. If Grace didn't help…

They hadn't talked since the night Dylan died. When Grace had finally spread her own brother's ashes a few days later, Molly hadn't gone to the funeral. And Grace hadn't come to Dylan's. Nobody had.

Molly hadn't put an obituary in the paper. People were calling him a criminal, for heaven's sake. She had kept the funeral private. All she wanted in the paper was an official apology from the sheriff's department.

The drive to the Cordero ranch didn't take long. By the time she pulled up the driveway, Skipper's shaking had quieted. Grace's car was there. A good sign. Molly beeped the horn.

Grace opened the front door, took one look at her face through the windshield and came running. "What is it? Is it Logan?"

"Skipper," Molly said as she opened the door and jumped from the car, relieved to see only concern on Grace's face instead of any kind of resentment.

She was right there helping. A good thing, since it took the two of them to carry the listless dog into the house.

Grace lay Skipper right on the living-room floor and ran her hands all over the dog. "Muscle spasms. What happened? Snake bite?"

"I think she ate something again."

"Vomited?"

"Yes."

Grace probed the dog's belly with her fingers. Skipper squirmed and gave a humanlike moan.

"Did she have any shakes worse than this?"

"Yes." And just as she said that, the dog started shaking harder again.

Grace looked into her mouth, at her tongue, then ran to the laundry room and came back with her medical bag, measured out some medicine and dribbled the liquid into Skipper's mouth little by little. She kept examining the dog while Molly shifted on her feet.

"So how are *you* doing?" Grace asked without turning around, probably to distract her from the panic that was filling her chest.

What was a safe topic? "I think I kind of went on a date."

That earned a look and a tentative smile. "Mo?"

"Kenny," she said quickly.

"Oh. Ryder said Mo was kind of keeping an eye on your place. I thought…" Grace hesitated, as if wanting to say something about him, but then seemed to change her mind and only said, "I'm glad you're getting out. It's about time you stopped punishing yourself for the past."

Her defenses, barely lowered, went right back up. "I wasn't punishing myself for anything."

"You deserve love. How many guys have you turned down over the years?"

She shrugged. "I was busy with Logan and the ranch." But part of her, deep down, thought she didn't deserve some fairy-tale happily ever after.

She'd messed up when she'd been young. And worse than that, she was responsible for her family's falling apart, for her father's death. Just because nobody knew her darkest secrets, it didn't mean she didn't carry that guilt.

Grace was running her probing fingers over Skipper's abdomen again. "You keep any heavy-duty pesticides lying around?"

"No." She wouldn't dare have poison with Skipper getting into everything. And her gardening was strictly organic, her biggest selling point.

Grace gave her a quiet look. "Have any enemies?"

A chill ran through her. "You think she was poisoned?"

"I'm pretty sure. I'd like to keep her for a few days."

Dismay and anger filled her chest. "Why would somebody hurt her?"

"Maybe Dylan—" Grace started to say, then stopped. No way could they discuss her brother.

Molly stood. "How much do I owe you?"

"Don't be ridiculous."

And then they had nothing to say. The night of Dylan's death stood like an unbreachable stone wall between them once again.

She thanked Grace for the help and drove home, worrying about Skipper, trying to figure out what this all meant. So people believed the lies and thought Dylan had turned bad. But why take it out on her? And even if someone was doing just that, what had Skipper ever done to anyone? She was the best dog in the universe.

She was still worrying about the dog when she reached home and spotted a pickup and trailer in her driveway. Looked as if Kenny had brought his horse. He was coming from the stable, talking on his phone.

Bum date or not, she was happy to see him. The two-hundred-dollar boarding fee was a welcome addition to the ranch's budget. Knowing she had that little extra money would make her sleep easier.

He ended the call and put the phone away when she pulled up. "I put Charlie in the stall you made ready for him. Much obliged. Missed your call last night. By the time I saw it, I didn't want to call you back. I figured you'd be asleep."

"I had someone sniffing around." She told him about

the man in her backyard, about the possibility that Skipper might have been poisoned. "At least *you* believe that Dylan was innocent. I really appreciate that."

"Whatever you need from me. I want to be there for you." He stepped closer. "I mean it."

"Thanks. And I'll take good care of Charlie. I promise. I'll have him out in the back corral. I'm going to keep him separated from the others for a couple of days, until they all get used to each other." They should be fine. She didn't have another stallion, just a gelding and a couple of mares, and her mares weren't in heat.

"I'll be stopping in to check on him. Want to make sure I ride him. He needs the exercise."

"Come and go as you please. If I'm not here and you want to ride, just go straight back. I'll probably be putting padlocks on the outbuildings, but I'll give you a key."

He shook his head with an apologetic smile. "I was supposed to bring those locks, wasn't I? Don't know where my mind is these days. Next time I come out, I'll have them. I promise."

"Thanks, Kenny."

"You need to be safe."

"I need to find a way to prove that Dylan was framed and had nothing to do with smuggling. Whoever is coming around probably believes Dylan was guilty, and the idiot is trying to mete out some vigilante justice. Or they figure there may be some drugs or whatever other contraband hidden on the property, left over from the smuggling—easy pickings."

Once Dylan was exonerated, people would no longer have a reason to bother her. So that was what she had to achieve and in a hurry.

Kenny reached out to take her hand, a sympathetic expression on his face. "Listen—"

Her stomach sank. She pulled her hands away. "Don't tell me they talked you into this idiocy. Dylan was framed."

"Of course he was. But I was thinking, too, and…he might have had some link to something. Maybe he didn't even know it was bad. Somebody asking him for a favor. You know how he was."

"He would help anyone if they asked him."

"The wrong kind of people could take advantage of someone with a big heart like he had."

"Exactly."

"If someone asked him to store something for them for a while…"

She stilled. "Like drugs?"

"That man here last night." Kenny patted her hand again. "Sure sounds like he was looking for something. And…" He looked uncomfortable again.

"What?"

"I don't want you to be offended. I'm not accusing Dylan of anything."

"What is it?"

"I heard something through the grapevine this morning. An old informant called in."

Cold spread through her chest. "About Dylan?"

"No. But this guy says the local drug runners are looking for a missing shipment."

"My brother was no drug runner."

"Of course not. I'm just saying someone could have asked him to store something and he might not even have known what it was."

"But there's nothing like that here. I would know."

He tilted his head. "Would you?"

She thought of the bags and bags of feed, hay bales, the unused haylofts she hadn't climbed in ages, the covered-up grease pit in the garage. It was probably full of rattlers. "Maybe not," she admitted reluctantly.

Kenny gave a slow nod. "We got time. How about I help you look around? If we find something, I'll take care of it. I'll take it in. Your name or your brother's name doesn't have to come up."

Gratitude filled her. "You really are a good friend, Kenny."

Chapter Five

Mo squinted against the sun as he drove down the road, coming in from border surveillance, deciding to drop by the Rogers ranch. He was talking on the phone with Jamie, who was at the office, and turned up the Bluetooth so he could hear him better.

"Tell me you're doing something exciting and I can be there in ten minutes. Tell me you busted someone."

They were all itching for action.

"Barely any movement. The shipments are definitely on hold."

"The big boss probably figured out surveillance was stepped up. We did take two tunnels out of commission."

Right. They'd covered that ground before. It made sense. Except... Mo tapped his fingers on the steering wheel as he rethought their theory.

"CBP does raids and surges all the time. The smugglers just move to another method. When border surveillance is stepped up, they switch to transporting contraband hidden in trucks, right through the checkpoints. When checkpoints get extra agents, they switch to swimming the river. When the river is monitored, they go to the tunnels. They don't just stop everything all at once."

"Okay," Jamie said on the other end. "So why the moratorium now?" He paused and spoke to someone in the office, away from the phone, for a second before getting back to Mo. "So, um, Ryder's in. He says Grace says Molly Rogers's dog was poisoned last night. He thought you might want to know."

Cold filled his stomach. "Thanks. I'll talk to you when I get in." He hung up and pushed down harder on the gas pedal.

He pulled up to the house, wrestled with the greeting committee, two dogs only, when he got out of his SUV, then went looking for Molly.

She was in the garden, harvesting summer squash, her curves encased in jeans shorts, the heels of her cowboy boots and her cowboy hat giving her an extra couple of inches in height. She was okay.

The tension in his stomach relaxed. She was better than okay. The top two buttons of her short-sleeved shirt were unbuttoned in deference to the heat, the bottom of the shirt tied in a knot at her waist.

He tried not to stare at her bare midriff. Nothing motherly about her today. With all her curves, she looked like a pinup girl.

She straightened, buttoned up the shirt one button and let the bottom down to cover her skin as she watched him approach. He wished she hadn't. *Focus on the business at hand.*

A flash of anger replaced the worry inside him. "Skipper was poisoned. Why didn't you call me?"

She pushed her hat out of her eyes.

Even as his fingers itched to reach for a stray strand of hair. He didn't.

"You're not a vet," she said. "There was nothing you could have done to help."

"Anything happens here, I want to know about it."

"I'm not involved in smuggling." Her full lips pressed into a scowl. "I thought we were past that."

"We are. I know you're not involved. But you're still linked to it through your brother." That sounded more official than saying that the thought of her coming to harm put a lead ball in his stomach. "You're still part of the investigation."

Fire came into her eyes as always when he brought up that subject. She picked up her bushel of squash and came out of the garden, closed the gate behind her. She marched up to the house, went in through the back door, leaving it open for him.

She set the bushel down just inside the door, then stepped out of her boots and took off her hat. "Kenny says whoever was out here last night might have been looking for drugs or something. Dylan had a lot of friends. One of them could have given him a package or whatever to keep. If that's what happened, Dylan wouldn't even have known what was in it." She blew the hair out of her eyes. "I checked around."

"Find anything?"

Her shoulders fell. "Nothing. And I looked hard. Kenny helped me, too. We looked for hours."

Kenny the ever-helpful.

He shifted closer. She smelled like sunshine and her lemon-verbena shampoo, the two of them standing barely two feet from each other in the narrow back entryway. He wanted to reach out and pull her to him.

"So Kenny and you…" He left the sentence hanging.

"Kenny went to school with Dylan," she said as she turned and walked away from him. "He's boarding his horse here now."

He waited, but she said nothing more, nothing about them seeing each other socially. He wasn't going to ask.

It was none of his business. "Are you seeing him?" The words snuck out anyway.

She stopped by the fridge and opened the door, but turned back. "He's a friend."

She looked into his eyes as she said that. He didn't think she was lying. Still, she might think Kenny was her friend, but Kenny wanted more. The way the sheriff had looked at her at Gordie's… The thought tightened the muscles in Mo's jaw.

Kenny seemed to be spending a lot of time here lately, he thought as he walked over to the kitchen table where she set out a glass of sun-brewed iced tea for him.

He liked sitting in her kitchen and drinking sweet tea. He could easily imagine doing a lot more of that. Doing other things, too.

Except, when his op was over, he would be out of here. He'd be going to Washington to work for the CIA, then probably out of the country on his first assignment.

To start something with Molly under the circumstances wouldn't be right. Despite the gossip, he knew what kind of woman she was—the family kind. She wasn't out looking for a temporary lover. She deserved nothing less than a husband, and a father to Logan, someone who would stick by her, help her run the ranch.

And Mo couldn't give her that. He had a schedule. CIA first, while he was young enough to do active duty overseas—another ten years, he figured. Then he would be transferred to desk duty in the States. That was the time when he would be looking to settle down and start a family.

Molly was great, but he wasn't there yet, wasn't ready. Which was why he needed to get the idea of kissing her out of his head.

If only it was that easy.

HE HAD THE KIND of presence that filled up a place. Mo in her kitchen drinking her iced tea and making appreciative noises created tingles in her stomach. She wished Kenny could do that—Kenny, whom she'd known forever, who was actually interested in her.

Kenny believed in her brother's innocence. Kenny would still be around next year and the next and the next. Kenny was a normal person, not part-owner of a multimillion-dollar company like Mo.

She'd done the "most eligible bachelor" thing. She'd fallen in love with the son of the richest man in town, let herself be blinded by her teenage crush and be thoroughly seduced by him.

When she'd told him she was pregnant, he refused to believe he was the father. He refused to have anything to do with her. He'd threatened to take her son away if she ever breathed his name in connection with paternity. And he had enough money to hire all the lawyers he needed to get the job done.

Rich people lived by a different set of rules than the rest of the world. They got what they wanted, any way they wanted it. Smartest thing to do was to stay out of their path. When you hooked up with someone like that, they had all the power. She would never let that happen again. She was not an impressionable seventeen-year-old anymore.

Whatever attraction she felt for Mo, she was more than capable of resisting it. She would never be more than a temporary plaything to him, to fill his time while here on assignment. When this job ended, he would go away and leave her heartbroken. She needed that like a rattler in her boots.

"Listen, I should—" She was trying to politely tell him that she needed to get back to work—these little moments in her kitchen had to end—but the phone rang before she could finish the sentence. She stepped over to the counter to pick it up.

"Hi, is this Ms. Rogers? I'm Betty from the principal's office."

Her whole body tightened in an instant. "Did something happen to Logan?"

"He's okay, but he was in a fight a little earlier. Mr. Talbot would like you to come in."

Not again. She squeezed her eyes shut for a second. "I'll be right there." She hung up then turned to Mo. "Sorry, I have to go."

He emptied his glass as he stood. "What happened?"

"Logan got in trouble at school for fighting." She glanced down at her clothes. Other than one minor smudge of dirt from the garden, they were passable. She hurried to the pegs by the back door and grabbed her purse.

"I'll go with you." Mo was right behind her.

"It's not necessary. It's—"

"Why don't I just come anyway?"

She didn't have time to argue with him. She pulled on her summer sandals and rushed through the door. He drove.

She didn't mind that. She was distracted—all the things that had been happening at the ranch, then Skipper and now Logan... "He's a good kid." Her tone came out defensive.

"I know."

"He's taking Dylan's death really hard."

Mo nodded, his SUV gobbling up the miles. He drove faster than she would have normally been comfortable with, but under the circumstances, she didn't mind.

They sat in silence as she worried.

"Find any tire tracks from the other night?" she asked eventually. "I keep forgetting to ask."

He nodded. "They led east for half a mile then cut back

to the road. I took some casts. Generic tires you can buy at any gas station. Not much of a lead."

She filled her lungs. "I just want everything to go back to normal."

"Give it time. Things will settle down." He slowed as they reached the school and pulled into the visitors' parking lot right by the front door.

She was unbuckling the seat belt even before he shut off the engine. "Thanks. You don't have to come in."

"I don't mind." He followed her to the principal's office.

Mr. Talbot was waiting for them. Logan, with a split lip, sat in the corner, his head hanging.

She wanted to rush up to him and ask if he was okay. She didn't. He had behaved badly, and he knew it. She wasn't about to coddle him. Positive reinforcement had to be reserved for positive behavior. Parenting was hard business.

He hung his head even deeper as the door closed behind them. "I'm sorry, Mom."

"Ms. Rogers." The principal stood, then looked at Mo.

"Moses Mann," Mo introduced himself. "Friend of the family. What happened?"

"A fight in the bathroom, apparently. The other child involved has already been sent home. Both boys are receiving suspensions for the rest of the week."

Molly bit her lip. "I'm so sorry. It's not like Logan at all. He's been having a hard time lately." They were going to have a long talk about this. Again.

"I know," Mr. Talbot agreed. "And from what I hear, he didn't start the fight. Regardless, we don't condone violence."

Logan stood and shuffled over to her. While she didn't approve of his actions, she hated the crushed look on his little face. She put her hand on his shoulder, wanting nothing more than to get out of there.

But Mo said, "Do you condone bullying?"

The principal frowned. "Of course not."

"Were you aware that Logan has been bullied on multiple occasions over his uncle's death?"

"Mr. Mann—"

"Would you mind sharing with us what steps have been taken so far to stop it?"

The principal swallowed. He was a head shorter than Mo and probably a hundred pounds lighter. And it wasn't just Mo's physique that was impressive. He could turn his voice into tempered steel, his eyes hard and cold in a way that really made you want to not mess with him. She knew that voice and look, had the bad luck to experience it in the interrogation room.

He kept on pushing. "Do you think it's wise to allow bullying to go on in your school and then punish the victim? Have you thought about what kind of message you're sending to the children? To their parents? Do you take the safety of your students seriously, Mr. Talbot?"

"Well, Mr. Mann—"

"The law does allow for self-defense."

"Of course."

"So there should be no reason at all for Logan's suspension. Seeing how he didn't start the fight."

A strained silence stretched between them.

"Yes. I think you're correct." Mr. Talbot adjusted his tie then looked at her. "You can, of course, still take him home for the rest of the day."

Since Logan did look as if he could use a little cleaning up, she said, "Thank you. I will." And watched as her son stared at Mo as if he was some hero straight out of the comic books, an expression very similar to the one he used to regard Dylan with.

She hoped she was controlling her own expression a

little better. She couldn't remember the last time some-one, other than her, had stood up for her son. The look on his smudged face told her how much that meant to him.

They stepped out of the principal's office just as the bell rang, kids filling the hallway. More than a few curi-ous glances were directed toward Mo and his commando swagger. He put a friendly smile on his face, then a hand on Logan's shoulder as they walked out.

The kids pulled back respectfully. Logan seemed to grow several inches.

She glanced at his split lip. "Are you okay?" That her son had been cornered in the bathroom broke her heart. Maybe Mo was right and it wasn't always possible to walk away from trouble. She didn't want Logan hurt.

"No big deal." He shrugged, playing the tough guy.

But he shouldn't have to. He shouldn't have to suck up a beating, and she shouldn't have to worry about sending him to school.

"If the offer still stands," she told Mo as they walked out, "maybe you could teach him just a little bit about how to defend himself."

"I'd be happy to. Hope you don't mind that I spoke up in there. Punishing Logan didn't seem right or fair."

She shook her head. Honestly, she could have kissed him.

"ANYTHING INTERESTING so far?" Mo asked Jamie over the radio the next morning.

The air shimmered in the heat, the ground nothing but dust. What few bushes and grass still clung to life weren't terribly impressive. His SUV left a pretty big dust cloud behind as he drove over the landscape. He was probably visible from miles away. He doubted he'd be catching any-one today.

CBP had their own patrols, few and far between, due to budget restrictions. Mo's team had been set up to provide a more comprehensive coverage for the section they were interested in.

"Caught a handful of people crossing this morning, all at separate locations. Just swam for it. Didn't look like part of the smuggling operation. They had no guides," Jamie told him.

"Mules?"

"They didn't carry anything. Swam across with the clothes on their backs."

Customs and Border Protection could deal with them, Mo thought and kept driving, keeping an eye out for anything out of the ordinary.

He was looking for floating devices hid in the bushes or signs that trucks had gone through here. They were looking for a bigger operation, an organized one, people who transported massive amounts of illegal cargo, the ones who would be bringing those terrorists and their weapons of mass destruction over.

He drove up an incline, and when he reached the top, the land stretched in front of him all the way to the Rio Grande. He parked the SUV next to Jamie's and they both pulled out their binoculars, Mo scanning the land to the left and Jamie to the right.

His attention was on the job, but he still had Molly on his brain. He had Molly Rogers way too much on his brain lately. He hoped she was doing all right. And Logan, too. The kid deserved a break.

"I think I see something," Jamie said after a minute. "Straight west. There's something in that gully."

Mo looked and saw a boxy shape, a glint of metal. "A car?" Hard to tell from here. He set his binoculars down and drove in that direction.

Once they were closer, he could make out a small truck. Bingo.

Mo checked his gun, called the find in to Ray, who was on office duty, giving his leg a rest so the cast could come off eventually.

The closer they got, the slower he drove. No signs of movement around the truck; the lettering on the side advertised flower delivery. On a regular road, nobody would look at it twice. Out here, however, there were no flowers and nobody to deliver to.

"Flat tire," Jamie said when they were only a hundred feet away.

That explained why the truck was sitting in the gully, the coolest spot around. The motor was running, probably for the air-conditioning in the cab.

"I sure hope there are no people in the back." The truck didn't have any cooling back there, from what he could see, no outside vent units. Mo stopped his car. "You go left. I go right." He checked his gun again before getting out.

Even at six in the morning, the heat was intense. Any hotter and the dirt would start melting. They sucked up the heat and rushed the truck from the back, one on each side.

The driver must have seen them in his side mirrors because he rolled his window down and started shooting.

"Drop your weapon!"

Mo shot back and kept running forward, dodging bullets as he went. He reached the door the same time as Jamie did on the other side. They both aimed their weapons at the man's head.

"Hands up! Throw out your weapon and get out of the cab!"

The man had no way to escape and he knew it. He only hesitated a second before complying. He swore up a storm in Spanish as he opened the door and dropped to the ground, then onto his knees.

His clothes were wrinkled and lived-in, his face unshaven. He smelled like beer. He shot a murderous look at Mo, but put his hands on the back of his head without having to be prompted.

"He knows the drill," Jamie said, coming around.

Right. Sure looked as if he'd run into trouble with law enforcement before.

"Who are you?" Mo asked in English first, then in Spanish, holding his gun on the guy while Jamie patted him down for hidden weapons. He came up empty.

The man kept quiet, looking straight in front of him. He was probably more scared of the people he worked for than the border patrol.

As Mo cuffed the driver, Jamie shot off the lock from the back of the truck. The gate creaked as it opened. "Empty," he called.

Mo dragged the man to his feet, took him over to his SUV and locked him in the back. Jamie was climbing into the back of the truck. Nothing but a couple of empty water bottles and a rag in the far corner. He headed for that, kicked it.

"Anything interesting?"

"Just a dirty shirt." He came back and jumped to the ground.

"Human cargo. He brought them over the border then let them off when the truck broke down."

Jamie nodded and scanned the ground, too stony for footprints here. He walked a few yards away and kept looking.

Mo pulled out his cell phone and called in the find, asked Ray to let CBP know to be on the lookout for illegals. A daylong hike could be deadly in this heat.

He walked up to the cab as he hung up, turned off the engine, found nothing but snacks and more empty water bottles. No registration papers for the truck or any other documentation in the glove compartment. He was willing to bet they weren't going to find ID on the driver, either.

He checked the GPS unit and hit pay dirt. "Last address entered was the Hullett sheriff's office," he called out to Jamie. "You take the driver in. I'm going to drive over and see Sheriff Shane."

He lucked out, caught the sheriff right in his office.

The man received him with a smarmy smile and an assurance of his full cooperation with whatever Mo's problem was, and listened as Mo filled him in on the truck. "Any idea why the GPS would be programmed for this office?"

"Now, don't you start on that." The sheriff glared at him, taking a toothpick from his mouth and shoving it into his shirt pocket. "Just because you can't do your job and now you're getting desperate, don't think you're gonna go after my people." It was pretty clear he was tired of outsiders meddling in what he thought of as his business.

"I'm just here to see if you might know what that GPS is all about." No sense pissing off the local law until he knew something for sure. But if the sheriff and/or his staff was dirty, he was going after them with a vengeance. "All I'm asking is your opinion."

The sheriff flashed him a hard look. "My guess is they were coming to someplace in town. Put the station in the GPS so if they get caught nobody is the wiser about their true destination."

Mo thought about that for a second. *Maybe.* "I wouldn't mind seeing whatever files you have on smuggling cases you've had over the years."

The sheriff's face darkened another shade. Not that surprising. Nobody liked it when strangers messed with their business.

Better put a positive spin on it. "I'm putting together some statistics for the budget recommendations we're writing up. Who knows, maybe Hullett will get a chunk of federal money."

The man didn't look overly excited, but he did nod after a second. "I'll have my secretary gather up what we have."

Mo slid his card across the desk. "She can email me the files. I'd really appreciate it."

He left the Hullett sheriff, thinking about the exchange, about what the chances were that the man was involved. He hated to think that someone sworn to uphold the law would trample his oath into the mud like that. Then another silver star caught his eye. The Pebble Creek sheriff going past the receptionist with a nod. A professional visit?

An annoyed frown crossed Kenny's face as he spotted Mo. "Moses Mann." He even said the name with derision.

"Sheriff Davis."

"I hear you've been spending time at the Rogers ranch."

Okay, he hadn't planned on bringing up the subject, but as long as the sheriff had... Mo gave the man a level look. "I hear you've been doing the same."

"Molly is a friend. I don't like the idea of her out there alone," the man said easily, but his gaze hardened. "I don't like the idea of her being harassed, either."

"My concern exactly," Mo countered.

"I thought you were supposed to be watching the border."

"That and the people who cross it with bad intentions."

"And how long is this assignment of yours?"

"As long as it's necessary."

"Is it? Necessary? I'd hate to see taxpayer money

wasted. I'm sure whatever you're investigating, Molly is not connected."

"Just keeping an eye on her to make sure she's safe."

"How about you let me worry about that?" The sheriff's gaze hardened.

Getting into a confrontation with him would serve no purpose. So, as much as it burned him, Mo simply nodded and walked away from the man.

He had to go back to the office, but he decided to go out to the ranch and check on Molly when he was finished. He hadn't seen her yet today. He wanted to make sure Logan had been okay going back to school.

That some bully would mess with the kid ticked him off.

He was going to offer support to Logan. He was absolutely not going to think about kissing Molly. He had no business starting something he couldn't finish. Sooner or later, he'd be leaving. Kenny had been right about that.

Chapter Six

Molly went around finishing up her evening chores, trying not to stare at Mo in her backyard as he trained with Logan.

"Okay. So if someone grabs you from behind—" he demonstrated "—you do what?"

Logan flawlessly executed the move he'd been taught.

"And if the kid comes from the front, kicking?"

Once again, Logan was quick to block.

"Punching?" Mo's impressive muscles flexed under his black T-shirt as he demonstrated the attack in slow motion.

She felt her temperature rise a degree or two as she watched him. Who looked like that in a simple T-shirt? *Seriously.*

Logan whooped with glee as he deflected the punch.

The dogs watched them with interest, too. Max from a safe distance, Cocoa doing her best to get in the way.

Mo was teaching self-defense moves only, not to attack, just to deflect blows.

"The goal is not to hurt your opponent. Just to let him know that you can and will defend yourself. You use as little force as absolutely necessary. They'll get the message, believe me."

Logan beamed. "Yes, sir."

"How about you call me Mo? All right, let's try the

moves a little faster," she heard him say as she went into the barn to do the milking.

She started with Nellie, since she was the fussiest one. She had a tendency to kick over the milk bucket when she was in a temper. But she did all right this time, looking back toward the door as if listening for Mo's voice outside.

He did have a nice voice, deep-timbered and masculine. His tone could cut in the interrogation room, but she was beginning to wonder if that was a learned skill. He hadn't talked like that to her since, and he was extra gentle with Logan.

She moved her milking stool over to Holly, disinfected her udder then went on with the milking. By the time she finished with all the cows, Mo and Logan were coming into the barn.

Logan was grinning from ear to ear, eyes wide with excitement. "Mom, want to attack me from the front?"

"Ah, how about a little later?"

"Why don't we give her a hand first?" Mo reached for the pails.

They processed the milk then Mo helped with the rest of her evening chores.

"You don't have to do that," she told him as he collected the eggs with Logan. "Although I do appreciate the help."

She was used to doing it alone. Dylan had too many businesses to give a hand with the day-to-day operations at the ranch.

"Actually," Mo said as they walked inside through the back door. He waited until Logan rushed off to the laundry room to wash his hands, before continuing, "I didn't just stop by to quickly check on you. I'd like to do a stakeout at the ranch tonight, if you don't mind."

A stakeout? "Did something happen today?"

Logan ran back. Mo stayed silent.

"Sure," she said after a moment. She wanted him to catch the bad guys so Dylan's name would finally be cleared. "Thanks."

"I'll be around, then." He turned to leave.

"Would you like to have dinner with us?" she asked on impulse as she moved to the sink to clean up. He had helped her so much today. And not just today, really.

"You don't have to feed me." But he was smiling.

He was sexy when he smiled. She used to think his torn eyebrow made him look fierce and threatening. Now she thought it just made him look interesting. Added character.

"It's just a couple of burgers. And we have plenty." Why was she nervous all of a sudden? It wasn't as if she was asking him on a date.

"Love a good burger. Thanks."

Her fingertips tingled from nerves. Okay, this was way crazy. He was helping her out, and she was feeding him in exchange. No big deal.

Since she didn't want him to see how flustered she was, she turned from him and busied herself with making dinner.

He came to help.

He sure had a way of filling up the kitchen.

"So how did you lose that eyebrow, anyway?" she asked, then couldn't believe she had.

He ran his finger over the uneven skin. "I can't really talk about that. Sorry."

"No, I shouldn't have pried," she apologized. Then wondered just what kind of work he did. But she didn't bring up the subject again, not in front of Logan. And there wasn't really another moment of silence for a long time anyway.

During dinner, Logan entertained Mo with stories of the animals around the ranch. And how once, when he was little, he'd found a lizard in the yard, was afraid the chickens would get it while he had to take his nap, so he put it in his pocket, then hid it in the microwave.

Mo paid rapt attention and laughed at all the right places in the story, melting her heart little by little.

Then they discussed video games at length. Pretty much sounded like another language to her. The only thing she understood was that her son was way impressed with Mo's gaming knowledge.

When Logan asked if he could read to Mo instead of her before bed, she wasn't even surprised. They were rereading Harry Potter in the evenings, had switched to Logan reading to her a while back, instead of the other way around, so he could practice his reading skills. He also read to the dogs on occasion, which they oddly liked, but that was another story.

She had cleaned up and put away the last of the dishes by the time Mo came back down, his large frame filling the old house's narrow staircase. Twilight settled outside. They were alone in the small kitchen, the scene suddenly oddly intimate.

If she ever had a husband, she imagined this might be the part when he would pull her into his arms, kiss her and then they would go upstairs together. She swallowed.

"Thanks again for dinner," Mo said.

He really was a lot more handsome than scary. His size no longer intimidated her, not when she saw how gentle he was with Logan and with the animals around the ranch.

"You're welcome." Her gaze fell to his masculine lips and something deep inside her tingled. "Does this mean you'll cut me some slack the next time you come to arrest me?" She'd blurted the first stupid question that came to her mind out of nowhere.

He did have the decency to look chagrined. "I didn't arrest you. I took you in for questioning. For what it's worth,

I don't think you had anything to do with smuggling in the area. I haven't for a while. Nobody is coming to arrest you."

"Good to know," she said inanely, then winced. *Oh, great. Shoot me now.* A sparkling conversationalist she was not. "Thank you for what you did for Logan," she added, suddenly unable to stop talking. "I want him to have a good childhood. I want him to grow up and be able to reach his dreams."

He watched her for a quiet second. "What are your dreams?"

The images that pushed into her mind were too unrealistic so she pushed them away. "For Logan to be happy and for Dylan to be exonerated."

"Nothing for you specifically?"

She didn't want to go there, so she went on the defensive. "How about you?"

He shrugged. "Getting on the next team, the next level up."

She had no idea what that would be. "CIA? FBI?"

He gave her a half smile that was full of mystery. Right. If he were preparing to be some grand spymaster, he couldn't exactly tell her, could he?

So his current assignment was a stepping stone for him. "Do you know when you'll be leaving?"

"Molly…" He stepped forward and was suddenly too close. His gaze bored into hers.

She stood there wide-eyed, frozen like an armadillo in the headlights. The whole world seemed to stop for a moment.

She was pretty sure he was going to kiss her, and the thought nearly made her jump out of her skin.

But instead, after another moment, he shifted from one foot to the other, then turned and walked away. "I'll be out there if you need me. Just call my cell."

Then he was gone, and she felt a sudden wave of dizziness. Probably because she hadn't remembered to breathe in the past five minutes.

OKAY, THAT WAS CLOSE. That couldn't happen again. She was alone and in possible danger and no way in hell was he going to take advantage of her like that. Even if he really liked her.

The ranch was growing on him, too. Odd for a city kid, Mo thought as he walked around outside. But Molly's place had a lot of old-country charm, everything as neat as a pin, the house filled with warmth. He couldn't not feel comfortable sitting at that kitchen table.

Even the outbuildings were— He caught himself and shook his head. Right. Because he kept coming back due to his extreme fondness for the outbuildings. *Not.*

The dogs came running up from the back to walk with him.

"I even like you two goofballs," he admitted as they stared at him, tongues lolling.

But most of all, he really, really liked Molly. Truth was, he was developing an extreme fondness for Molly Rogers. Maybe even more than simple liking. He wanted her, that was for sure. His body was clear on that every time they were in the same room together.

And when they weren't together, he kept thinking about her. That was new. He wasn't the type to obsess over a woman. But she was different, had a different effect on him than the women he'd dated. Not that he'd had a great many relationships. His job didn't leave much time for that.

He'd always wanted family, just never thought it was time yet. Not for another ten years, according to the master plan.

Not that he knew how he would go about it once the time

did come. His experience with family had been his foster father and four brothers. His foster mother had died early on of cancer. The father, a retired Marine, ran the house like boot camp after that. The five boys definitely needed the discipline. He'd raised them well. But something had always been missing, and not until now had Mo realized what it was.

Motherly softness.

What Molly had here at the ranch, her gentle care of her son and even the animals, of which every single one had a name, down to the last scrawny chicken, was special. There was something here that drew him irresistibly, and it went beyond the fact that her amazing curves made his palms itch or that her kissable lips made him space out midthought, or that Logan was a great kid, one he wouldn't have minded spending more time with.

Of course, she probably couldn't wait to get rid of him. All she wanted was for her life to go back to normal. She'd said as much more than once.

Mo checked the outbuildings, walked through the stables, patted the horses. Sonoma, a young bay, snorted at him in greeting. The animals were starting to get to know him. He looked in at the new horse in the back. That one had to be Kenny's. He patted him, too. That he didn't like his owner had nothing to do with the animal.

He checked every stall then moved outside, Max and Cocoa escorting him all the way to his pickup. Skipper was getting better, according to Ryder, who visited Grace Cordero pretty much every day. Looked as if Ryder and Grace had something good, something real.

Mo squashed the beginning of some weird longing that thought awakened inside him. Ryder was ready for that next step. Good for him. Mo wasn't. He wanted to make it to the CIA. He wanted to make his father proud.

He started the engine and drove toward the fields instead of the main road. He pulled into the nearest mesquite grove, shut down the car and pulled out his binoculars. He could see the whole ranch from there, making it the perfect surveillance point. He scanned the house and the yard—everything was quiet.

Only one light was on in the house, Molly's bedroom. A shadow crossed behind the curtains. Stopped. She reached to the top button on her shirt and Mo swallowed hard. Then she stepped out of sight, and he didn't know whether to be relieved or disappointed.

He trained his binoculars elsewhere in case she came back to the window. She had no idea he was in the mesquite grove, in straight line of sight. He didn't want to invade her privacy.

He scanned the yard again, the outbuildings. Nothing but the two dogs moved. According to Molly, unless there was lightning and thunder, they preferred to sleep outside.

She'd kept them inside since Skipper had been poisoned, but he'd asked her to let them out tonight. If someone was sneaking around, they would signal. And this time, he was here to make sure nothing bad would happen to them.

But the dogs seemed relaxed, Max settling in to sleep, Cocoa patrolling the grounds.

Mo settled in for a long night, too. Some of his teammates hated surveillance. He didn't mind it. He liked quiet. He was comfortable being alone with his thoughts.

Except, this time, his thoughts kept returning to Molly Rogers.

A little after midnight, the light came on in her window. Maybe she was going to the bathroom. Then the light came on in Logan's bedroom. And stayed that way.

Mo glanced at his phone on the passenger seat next to him. If she was in trouble, she would call.

Unless she couldn't…

Someone could have gotten in through the front.

No. The dogs would signal.

Except it wasn't impossible to get by two dogs who were sleeping in the backyard. Cocoa and Max were stretched out next to each other.

Mo quietly slipped from the pickup, making sure he had his phone and his gun. If someone was out there, he didn't want to tip the guy off by turning on the motor or the lights. So he ran forward on foot, keeping to what little shadows the landscape provided.

The dogs woke up as he neared, came to check him out. He pushed them away and stole to the back door. It took less than thirty seconds to pop the old lock with the help of his knife.

He was just inching through the kitchen when Molly came down the stairs in that lavender silk nightgown that played a starring role in his dreams lately.

First she screamed, then she threw a heavy water glass at his head. He ducked just in time.

"It's me," he said quickly. "Are you all right?"

"Mom?" Logan called from upstairs.

"Spider," she called to him, then whispered to Mo, "What are you doing in here?"

"Saw your light come on." He picked up the glass that had luckily landed on the cushioned window seat. "You got a good arm."

"How did you get in?"

He shrugged. "I know a few useful tricks." He held out the empty glass. "What happened?"

"He had a nightmare. He's settled down now. I just wanted a cold drink."

But when she turned, he could see at last that she was more shaken than she'd let on, her eyes filled with worry.

"A dream about bullies?"

She shook her head as she walked to the fridge. "He dreamed he was out in the fields, far from the house, lost and alone." She filled her glass and held out the tea pitcher. "I think it's because of Dylan's death."

He picked another glass from the dish drainer and held it out for her to fill. "I think you're right."

He'd had those dreams, different variations, when he'd first found out he'd been abandoned by his parents as a baby, and then when his foster mother had died. He kept having dreams that his foster father would somehow disappear, too, and he would be alone in the world. He used to wake up in a dark terror, shaking.

"Do you see why it's so important for me to clear Dylan's name? I want to at least give Logan that."

He wished that was possible. But both she and Logan needed to somehow deal with Dylan's death, and the truth. Because his name wasn't going to be cleared. He wanted to fix this for her somehow, hated that he couldn't.

The shaft of moonlight that fell across her face revealed the desperation in her eyes.

He was here to protect her, Mo reminded himself. Touching her, in any way, would be plain stupid and completely inappropriate, even if the protection detail wasn't official. But no matter what he told himself, nothing seemed to work.

He sat his glass down and pulled her into his arms.

SHE COULDN'T REMEMBER the last time anything felt half as good as it did to be held by Moses Mann.

He was big and strong and made her feel protected. Nothing was going to get through him to get to her. She felt safe in his arms and comforted.

And not alone.

She'd felt so alone since her brother's death.

Logan was the light of her life, but Logan was different. She was responsible for Logan. Dylan had been another adult, more of a partner in life's small troubles. It really was nice to have another adult around again.

A week ago, she couldn't wait to see the last of Moses Mann. Now she dreaded the day when he would leave. It seemed impossible that she could come to trust him this fast. And her growing attachment to him, too, was disconcerting. She normally had better self-control than this.

She looked up and found him looking down at her. Even in the semi-darkness she could see the heat in his eyes. He wasn't touching her in any sexual way, offered nothing but comfort, but the heat was there between them anyway.

She didn't look away.

And then, in the blink of an eye, somehow everything changed. Slowly, giving her plenty of time to protest, he lowered his lips and brushed them over hers.

Oh, wow. Was this really happening?

That Moses Mann would be kissing her seemed surreal on some level. He was so…strong and brave and a millionaire and worldly—everything she wasn't. She was just a plain country girl.

They were so completely wrong for each other. Unfortunately, her hormones didn't give a damn. Need punched into her like never before, something big and scary and overpowering and completely unexpected.

For a second, she was too startled to do anything.

Then it was too late to resist, the flood of need washing over her completely. As if a dam had broken, she responded to the kiss with every fiber of her being. A low moan escaped her throat, her hands dug into his arms, her lips parted under his.

She burrowed against him, needing, wanting.

He tasted like the sweet tea he'd just drank. Like sunshine and, at the same time, the opposite—something dark and excitingly male. He tasted just right, frankly, after years of sexual repression and frustration.

So she wasn't dead below the neck like she'd told herself all these years, she thought, dazed, and as his tongue slow danced with hers, she swam with the pleasure.

Chapter Seven

She filled his senses. Her curves pressed to him, woke up his body and then some. The passion that exploded from her damn near took Mo's breath away. This was it, his instincts said, the real Molly, the one she took great pains to hide.

The grounded country girl, the good mother, the loyal sister he respected and was attracted to. The passionate woman he couldn't resist.

And, with everything he was, he wanted her.

But she pulled away suddenly, her hands pressed to her cheeks, her eyes round with embarrassment.

"I'm so sorry," she muttered. "I don't know why I did that. I'm really sorry." Then she turned on her heel and ran up the stairs, leaving him standing and staring in the middle of her kitchen.

He felt as if a tank had run him over.

He wanted to go after her, wanted to convince her that they both needed more of what they'd just shared. But he was pretty sure her speedy retreat upstairs meant no. And his foster father's many lessons included one on situations like this. When a lady said no, a real man accepted it and walked away. No pushing.

Even if it killed him. Even if in every other area of his life he'd been trained to push until he achieved his objective.

He ran his fingers through his crew-cut hair, considering dumping his remaining iced tea over his head. He could have used a little cooling off. But gaining perspective wasn't an easy thing with just a few steps separating them.

Steps he shouldn't take.

Their situation was pretty tricky. She was in trouble. He'd come to protect her, not to seduce her. Better put a little space between them right now.

He went outside, locking the doggie door to keep Max and Cocoa inside. They could guard the house while Mo took on the rest of the property.

He checked the outbuildings again and wouldn't let himself think about that kiss. No signs of anyone sneaking around while he'd been inside. All the animals were peaceful, all the doors closed and barred as he'd left them.

He didn't go back to his truck. He climbed up to the barn's hayloft. The old boards had enough gaps between them that he could see out in every direction, aided by the moonlight. An easy job, really, lying in the hay. It beat walking the border and having to worry about stepping on rattlers or being ambushed by smugglers.

Half his team was on patrol duty tonight, the other half on break. Even commando soldiers needed sleep. He was on break. Technically. But he didn't like leaving Molly alone at night. He wished she'd move into Hullett already.

He wished they were still in her kitchen, kissing. As much as he didn't want to think about that, he did, quite a bit, as he waited. Dawn was about ready to break when he heard some noise from down below that didn't come from the cows.

He listened more carefully to the slight scratching. A mouse?

No, something bigger. He eased toward the ladder, taking each step slowly so as not to rustle the hay. The scratching stopped. One of the cows, Nellie, turned to look at him and flicked some flies off her back with her tail.

He stood still in the shadows and waited. A minute or so later, the scraping sound returned. He could hear it better now, well enough to be able to tell where it was coming from: the small equipment room in the back where Molly kept her barn tools.

He stayed in the shadows as he moved forward, pulling his gun, ready.

The door, which had been closed before, now stood open. He eased his way over, saw a man inside with his back to the door, tapping the floorboards.

Mo stuck his gun behind his back, into his waistband. Better to take the bastard down by hand than shoot him. Dead men didn't talk, and he needed information. They needed to know who he was, who he worked for and what exactly he was looking for here.

He vaulted forward and crashed into the guy with his full weight. They slammed against the wall then went down, the both of them groaning.

Fist to the chin.

Grab the man's gun.

Toss it.

So far so good.

The intruder had plenty of muscle and knew how to use it, but Mo had managed to startle him. They grunted in unison as Mo tried to flip the man, get his hands behind his back so he could snap on the plastic cuffs he always carried.

Damned if the bastard didn't twist away at the last second. He put up a good fight, cursing alternatively in Spanish and English, both of them breathing hard once they'd rolled around a couple of times, smacking into the wall and various pieces of furniture, rolling over a pitchfork that nearly took out Mo's eye.

He had to put all his combat skills into play before he finally got the upper hand. With his knee in the middle of the guy's back, he used his whole weight to keep the man down while he twisted his arms back and finally snapped on the plastic cuffs. Just as he heard a footstep behind him.

He twisted, reaching for his gun. Too late.

The newcomer already had his weapon drawn.

THE DOGS WERE going mad at the back door, waking her from a perfectly good dream, in which she had a perfectly good man in her bedroom. Perfectly naked. Molly couldn't see his shadowed face, but his wide shoulders and massive build looked suspiciously like Mo's.

She opened her eyes and groaned at the ceiling in protest as she came awake. The dogs' barking grew more frenetic. Then she remembered that Mo was out there tonight.

Oh, God. Had they really kissed? She'd thrown herself at him like a starving woman. Embarrassment and heat filled her at the memory, in equal measure. Then worry, as the dogs kept barking.

She reached for her cell phone on the nightstand and dialed his number.

He didn't answer. And suddenly all sorts of bad premonitions filled her. She yanked on her bathrobe and ran downstairs. Grabbed her rifle from the gun cabinet. Pushed back the dogs, who were fighting to get out the back door as soon as she opened it.

"You stay here. Go to Logan," she told Cocoa as she went outside with Max. She locked the door behind her. Her dogs were sweet, but if anyone went after her or Logan, she was pretty sure they would have something to say about it, would probably give their lives to protect their humans. Max had gone up against an ocelot a couple of years ago to protect her and her horse when she'd been out riding.

The dog ran straight to the barn, still barking, so she followed, a little more carefully, keeping to cover.

"Mo?" she called out from the door.

Max had gone into the back room and stayed in there, quiet.

"Mo!" She raised her voice, clutching her weapon. She didn't dare turn on the lights, wasn't sure who might be in there, waiting for a chance to take a shot at her.

Then Mo called "In here" from the back.

She flipped on the lights then, but saw nobody save the cows. She ran to Mo.

He was sitting in the middle of the floor, rubbing his chest, looking dazed. Max was licking his face, doing the whole "I'll lick you back to health and happiness" routine dogs did so well.

Mo's face was bruised, his clothes scuffed.

"What happened?"

"There were two men." He groaned as he pushed to his feet. Patted Max. "Got me with a Taser."

"What?" She swung back toward the open barn, keeping her rifle ready. "When?"

He rubbed his chest again. "I think I blacked out a little." He looked at her rifle. Frowned. "You should have stayed inside."

She braced a hand on her hip. "Because you're the big bad man and I'm just a little helpless woman?"

He glared. "Have you ever shot anything bigger than a rattler?"

Okay, not really. But she didn't want to seem totally incompetent. "The bigger they are, the easier to hit, right?"

"The bigger they are, the worse they fight back." He pulled out his cell phone and dialed. "I'm going to call in my team to take some fingerprints."

She felt terrible that he'd gotten hurt on her property

and wanted to help, but she was at a loss as to how to do that. He wasn't like Logan, who could be set to rights with a hug and a kiss and some ice cream.

Yet she wanted to go up to him anyway, up real close…

She backed away. "I need to go back inside. Logan's in there alone."

"I'm coming with you." He followed her as he talked to someone on the other end, reporting in.

He went inside the house first, looked around while she made sure Max came back with them. He checked every door and window, every room upstairs, while she looked in on Logan, then plodded back down the stairs.

"Doesn't look like anyone tried to get in here," he told her.

"Logan is sleeping." She sank into one of the kitchen chairs. "Why do they keep coming?"

He thought for a long second. "They think you have something they want."

"I don't have anything."

"Maybe you don't know you have something."

Her jaw muscles tightened. "We've been over this with Kenny. Dylan wasn't hiding any contraband. He wouldn't. He wasn't into smuggling. And even if he was, he would never bring anything here and put Logan and me in danger."

"Wish I knew what it was," he said. "Searching for it would go easier if we knew we're looking for a truckload of weapons or a suitcase full of money."

She shook her head. None of this made any sense. Dylan didn't have a suitcase full of money. If he had, he wouldn't have mortgaged the ranch.

Mo rubbed his thumb over his damaged eyebrow, looking deep in thought, then he raised his head and considered her for a few seconds before he spoke. "I don't want you to stay here. For the time being. Especially at night. I can't be here every night, and you shouldn't be alone out in the middle of nowhere with Logan."

"I'm not going anywhere," she said on reflex, even if she knew he was right.

"How about we consider this for a minute?" he said patiently.

"Fine." She glared at him. "Be completely reasonable in an emotional moment. Just like a man."

The corner of his mouth tilted up.

She so didn't want to leave. She loved the ranch. It was the only thing she knew. But as much as she hated the idea of moving, for her son's safety she would. She would do anything for Logan.

She nodded with reluctance. "I'll be getting Dylan's apartment the day after tomorrow. Kenny talked to Shane about it. He's going to get me the keys."

He seemed to weigh her words. Then he said, "I've seen the apartment. Not exactly high security."

"I can't afford Secret Service detail." She couldn't afford to rent the apartment, either, and Dylan only had the rent paid until the end of the month. "You could stay at my place," Mo said carefully. "You can still come back here during the day to take care of the animals. I can make sure someone from the team is here when you come."

She stared at him. *His place.*

Okay. What did that mean? As a friend? As more? They *had* kissed. Or was he offering safety in an official capacity?

She could just barely picture herself leaving the ranch. Moving in with Mo… She needed to know what he meant by it. "I'm guessing you don't offer room and board to every person you interrogate."

A wry smile stretched his masculine lips. "Pretty much

never. I haven't even had the guys on the team over." He shrugged. "I'm not exactly a social butterfly. More of a loner, actually."

"Sounds like you like your private life private." She did, too. She liked living out here in the middle of nowhere. She'd never lived anyplace else.

Since she'd had Logan right after high school, she had never gone away to college. She'd received her agricultural-management degree through one of those low-residency programs where she only had to go on campus twice a year to take her exams. And the college had day care for young mothers during those residencies.

Her dream had been to create a preservation education operation, growing and preserving rare and heirloom fruits and vegetables and allowing various colleges to hold open-air lectures on her land. But Dylan had said it couldn't be done. They simply didn't have the resources.

She could have applied for grants, but he'd gotten upset when she'd mentioned that. He was proud that way, didn't like the idea of his sister going around begging, hat in hand.

And it was fine. She loved her animals, loved her garden, had a lot more time to spend with Logan than if she was running a serious operation. As long as she was on the ranch, she was happy.

Living at Mo's place…

The passionate kiss they'd shared earlier filled her mind, making her lips tingle. She felt awkward just sitting with him in her kitchen. What would it be like to spend serious time together? Could she pretend that she didn't like him as much as she really did?

"I'm on duty almost around the clock," he said, as if reading her thoughts. "And I'll come by at night as much as I can. I want to catch those men if they come back. You would pretty much have the place to yourself."

Odd how something could set a person more at ease while being disappointing at the same time. So, going to Mo's place... What choice did she have? Not much if she wanted to keep her son safe.

"I don't want harm to come to you or Logan," he said, underscoring her thoughts.

Which meant what? That they meant something to him?

Her insides began tingling again.

"Okay." She closed her eyes for a second. "Thank you."

His shoulders relaxed, the smile on his face widened. He looked pleased as punch, while she worked hard to hide her misgivings. He was about to say something, but then the dogs barked and soon they heard the sound of a car coming up her driveway.

He went to the window and looked out. "It's Jamie and Shep. I'll go talk to them. You stay here."

She watched from the window as he led his friends to the barn and they disappeared inside. She fed the dogs breakfast to keep them quiet, but Logan woke up anyway and plodded down the stairs, bringing his handheld "Calvin Cat Counting" game with him.

He was even more obsessed with the games now that he knew Mo's connection. He was quickly developing some hero worship for Mo that had started after the school incident and martial-arts training. It worried her a little. She didn't want Logan to fall for Mo so completely, not when she knew Mo wouldn't be staying.

A worry for another day. She had plenty of other things on her plate today. She put a big smile on her face. "Hey, you. How about breakfast?"

He sat in his chair and yawned as he nodded, looked toward the window and saw the men in the backyard. "Mom? Who is that?"

"Some of Mo's friends. They're working in the barn."

She didn't want to scare her son with details. "Guess what?" She widened her smile as she got out the bowl to make pancakes. "Mo invited us to visit with him."

He brightened immediately. "I bet he has a lot of video games."

"I bet he does. And it's not just any visit. It's a sleepover. Probably for a few days."

Logan jumped from his chair, looking as if someone had just told him Santa Claus was coming early. "I'm not going to school?"

"I'm pretty sure the school bus stops there, too." She shook her head.

His enthusiasm waned a little, but not by much. "Can I pack now?"

She laughed as she stirred the pancake mix. "I think packing can wait until after breakfast."

So they ate together and Logan talked about nothing but going to Mo's place. They rarely went away, mostly because they had little family to visit, and also because somebody had to be here for the animals.

Since it was admin day, no school, they did go upstairs to pack. Logan finished first. She spent an eternity agonizing over which clothes to take. She didn't want to look like a country bumpkin in front of Mo. Stupid vanity, she told herself and nearly packed her rattiest work clothes. But at the last minute, she folded her nicer dresses into the suitcase instead.

The extra SUV was gone from the driveway by the time she came downstairs. Mo was just coming in.

"Everything's taken care of. I'll help you do morning chores before we leave."

And he did. And, Lord, that was nice, not just the help but the company. He was a quiet man, didn't talk her ear off like Kenny. Quiet, but strong and efficient. He figured out everything right quick, too. She didn't need to explain a thing.

As he mucked out the stalls, nobody would have guessed that he was some gaming-empire millionaire. She stared at him, just a little, before she caught herself. She'd been worried about Logan, but was she falling just as fast for Mo?

"Done here." He leaned the pitchfork against the wall. "I'll just wheel this out back." He grabbed the wheelbarrow.

"Thanks." She looked after him as he went, then busied herself with the cows, even as her thoughts kept lingering on Mo.

He seemed to be the type of man who could fit in anywhere, do anything and be good at it because he paid attention and gave top effort. He didn't put on airs. He could have been dressed all in Armani, but wore simple clothes and didn't mind getting them dirty.

By the time the chores were done, she nearly talked herself into the fantasy that they weren't so different after all, that maybe some relationship between them could be possible while he was here.

That thought went right out the window when they finally arrived at his apartment in Hullett an hour later.

Logan walked around wide-eyed, touching everything, exclaiming over something every second. She felt the same, although held herself back. But only just. She was more than a little shell-shocked.

"You, um, have a very nice place."

The understatement of the year. He rented in the fanciest building in town, a historical hotel on Main Street once owned by an oil baron. The whole top floor had been the baron's private living space. Now Mo was staying there.

"Sit," she ordered her dogs and pointed to a corner, hoping they wouldn't mess up anything. Thank God they weren't chewers. She couldn't afford to replace as much as a doormat here.

"They'll be fine." Mo was smiling at her.

"This is very fancy," she said weakly.

"Didn't want it, didn't need it." He set down her suitcase and raised his hands palms out, in a defensive gesture. "I came to rent something small. Turns out the manager is somewhat of a gaming buff. He gets every gaming magazine. My name was familiar to him and he asked. I didn't want to lie to his face. All he had to do was look it up on Google."

Of course, in the gaming circles the Mann name was probably famous. And the manager would insist that Mo take the penthouse apartment, the best they had.

She couldn't imagine who else would ever have money to rent the place. Visiting politicians? The pope?

He moved farther in, seemingly oblivious to all the fanciness. "Let me show you around so you and Logan can get settled in."

He led her through the large living room, where the furniture was modern and well made. "At least it came furnished," he said. "Otherwise, I'd be probably sleeping in a sleeping bag on the floor."

Logan stared at the longhorn armchairs, actually made with cattle horns. The leather couch was as big as Texas. It looked like something from one of those high-end home-design magazines she couldn't afford to read.

The place had a full kitchen with top-of-the-line appliances, although they were so fancy she wasn't sure she'd know how to operate them. She drew a hand over the smooth granite countertops, pure luxury.

"The place came with two guest bedrooms all set up." Mo led them forward.

She followed him hesitantly, already overwhelmed,

while Logan plowed ahead. The first bedroom had a flat-screen TV of immense proportions. In front of the TV stood some sort of a console, a leather armchair with a dashboard built in. Looked like the captain's chair from the USS *Enterprise*.

"My brother sent it over last week. Some new game he wants to put out. Space cowboys." He shrugged. "Not exactly my area of expertise. He's the programming genius. But from the beginning he insisted that I get a vote on everything. So I'm supposed to evaluate the *experience*." He shook his head. "Maybe Logan could help?"

"Mom," Logan squealed. "Can I have this room? Please?" He actually had his hands clutched together in front of him, his eyes as big as Ping-Pong balls.

"Sure," she said weakly. She had no idea how they were ever going to repay Mo for all this.

She backed out of the room. Logan stayed behind, diving for the game console. And where she wouldn't have had any idea how to even turn the thing on, he had a game going in less than thirty seconds.

Mo moved down the hallway, stopped in front of the next room. "This could be your room, if it's acceptable."

A four-poster bed dominated the space, the room decorated in grays and earth tones, sumptuous and sophisticated at the same time. So unlike her. And yet she was completely in love with it. She felt like a kid at the state fair and had an idea that she probably looked just as amazed and wide-eyed as Logan.

Mo stepped aside so she could walk into the room. "Do you need anything? All you have to do is push the number-one button on the phone for concierge."

Concierge. "I think we'll be fine."

"Bathroom is right next door."

She stayed where she was. She didn't want to see the

bathroom. It probably had a marble Jacuzzi or something. She could only deal with so much at once.

"I'll leave you to settle in. I'm going to go into the office for a while. My hours aren't exactly regular," Mo said with a smile that said he was happy to have her here and, at the same time, that he'd be happy to have her.

Heat crept up her neck.

"Call me if you need anything."

What else could she possibly need? The suite had everything but a private butler. She'd never seen anyplace like it. That Mo lived here boggled her mind more than a little. The gap between them suddenly widened to a giant gorge. She nodded and watched him leave.

They were so not in the same league.

He strode to the front door, but then suddenly stopped and came back. "One more thing."

Her heart leaped. God, don't let him kiss her. She was so overwhelmed, she wasn't sure she could resist.

But instead of trying to make a move on her, he hurried around the apartment, reached under furniture, behind sofa pillows, into a kitchen cabinet and gathered up half a dozen guns of all sizes. He carried them to an abstract painting on the wall that turned out to be a safe and locked them in there.

"I don't want these within reach with Logan here," he said as he moved to leave again. Then stopped again.

He reached into his pocket and handed her a key. "I'll get another one for myself from downstairs. Make yourselves at home. Feel free to use the room service."

And then he kissed her, a lingering brush of his lips over hers before he strode out the door, leaving her staring after him.

She was pitiful. And he was…

Room service. Just like that. Was that how he ate? On

a daily basis? A day of that probably cost more than her weekly grocery bill.

"Mom, it has alien cowboys! Want to see?" Logan called from his room.

"In a second, honey."

She took in the place, more carefully this time, feeling more overwhelmed by the minute.

She and Mo were from different worlds. The kiss had meant nothing. She sank into the nearest chair as dismay filled her. Girls like her were nothing but playthings to men like him.

She'd learned that lesson early and wasn't likely to forget. She'd fallen in love, let herself be seduced, then had been cast aside the day she'd found out she was pregnant. Rich men wanted women for entertainment. Mo wouldn't want more than that from her.

Oh, God, she thought, feeling sick to her stomach. She'd done this before. Mikey had dazzled her with his money and extravagant gifts. He'd told her how much he'd cared for her. But all of that had been a setup.

And she'd almost fallen for it again. She felt so disappointed, she nearly choked on the feeling. Then she gathered herself and stood. She wasn't an impressionable young girl anymore, ripe for the plucking.

"All right. Let's see how those aliens fight." She headed back to Logan, thinking about her own battles.

She might have moved into Mo's apartment, but if he thought she was just going to waltz straight into his bed, too, he had another think coming.

Chapter Eight

Mo filed his reports and was on his way out of the office to stop by the jail again, this time to talk to the driver they'd caught by the border, when Ryder came in.

"Can I see you for a sec?" Mo gestured with his head toward the interrogation room, the only room in the office that had a door. The rest was open space with enough desks for the six-man team.

"Sure." Ryder followed him.

He was looking at Mo with expectation. "Everything okay?"

Mo scratched the back of his neck, not entirely comfortable. "So, about Molly Rogers."

"You got something on her?"

"She has nothing to do with anything. Thing is…" He paused, then bit the bullet. "I moved her and her son to my place at the hotel."

Ryder's eyebrows slid up his forehead.

Mo thought how to best word his explanation. "She keeps getting night visitors. She has an eight-year-old son. They're out there alone."

"She could have gotten her own room at the hotel."

Mo cleared his throat. "She's not that well-off financially."

"She has to have some friends."

She probably did. Although some of the people in town looked down on her, there were plenty of nice folks in Hullett. "If whoever keeps searching her place decides that whatever he's looking for is not there, they could come after her. She's safest at my place."

Ryder raised an eyebrow. "With you?"

Right. Slippery ground. "I'm never at the apartment. I'm either here or looking for crossing points on the border. For the next few days, I'm going to spend as many nights as I can at the Rogers ranch, see if I can catch whoever keeps going back there."

Ryder rubbed the bridge of his nose. "I know there's a certain irony here, considering Grace and me, but I have to ask…do you have an interest in Molly Rogers beyond the professional?"

Mo shoved his hands into his pockets. He wasn't used to talking about stuff like this. But Ryder was team leader and he had a right to know where this was going, if it would distract from the mission. Oh, hell. He filled his lungs.

"I don't really know. I want her and her son to be safe. And then—" He shook his head. "I have no idea what she wants."

Maybe Ryder could give him some tips. Ryder had managed to win Grace over, and Grace Cordero was one tough cookie.

But all he gave Mo was a sympathetic look. "Rather go into armed combat myself than try to figure out a woman."

Mo nodded. At least Grace was a soldier. She and Ryder had that in common.

Molly Rogers seemed like a whole different world to Mo. He was pretty much a killing machine, usually surrounded by violence on a daily basis. She was a mother, surrounded by chickens.

What did he know about women anyway? His birth

mother had tried to drown him. His foster mother had died when he'd been a kid. He never had sisters.

But he knew enough to know that Molly was special. She would be worth any effort to win. If only the timing of all this didn't suck so much. But maybe he could work on the timing. They had weeks before the planned terrorist crossing, if their intel was right. And even after the capture, more weeks would pass while they wrapped up everything here.

They needed to run down every last person involved, to make sure something like this couldn't happen again. His team was determined to secure the hundred-mile section of the border that they'd been trusted with.

"Is this going to be a problem?" He didn't define what "this" was. He had no idea what to call the instant attraction—at least on his part—between them, and those spectacular kisses, which he hoped would soon be repeated. "She's no longer a person of interest."

Ryder thought that over. "We're hunting criminals here. Terrorists. If someone figures out who we are, if they come after us, everyone connected to us could be in danger. Which is why I'm keeping my relationship with Grace under wraps as much as possible."

And Grace, after several tours overseas as an Army medic, could defend herself. Molly, on the other hand…

Mo rolled his shoulders. He hadn't thought about that. "I don't want Molly and her son in danger."

Ryder's face grew somber. "Then don't put her in any."

Easier said than done. "She's fine at my place. I secured it when I moved in. Reinforced the door with Kevlar. Nobody comes through that door unless they're let in. But while Logan is at school, she'll be at the ranch, taking care of her garden and her animals. I want some sort of protection for her."

"She'll get it. We'll make sure someone is out there with her while she's working. Her ranch is connected to our investigation. I can justify expanding some manpower there."

"I appreciate that."

Ryder shook his head. "Grace is worried about her, too."

They talked for another minute or two, then went about their business. Ryder needed to plan the schedules for the following week. Mo headed over to the county jail. After that, he'd take Molly and Logan out so she could do her evening chores at the ranch, then take them back to the hotel. Then he would return to the ranch to lie in wait, should any bad guys stop by during the night.

"I'll be back in the morning," he told Jamie and Shep, who were working on their computers.

"Another stakeout?" Jamie asked.

"Ready for more electroshock therapy so soon?" Shep ribbed him. "Hoping it'll curl your hair?"

"Very funny. Want to see how you'd like a couple of hundred volts between your ribs?" he offered.

The friendly taunting didn't really bother him. Not when Ryder had as good as given his approval. Molly would get team protection, too. And she was living at his place. He knew a grin was spreading across his face but didn't care.

He walked through the office then outside into the heat. He pushed Molly out of his mind and organized his thoughts around what he needed to do next. He needed to get the truck driver talking. They needed the name of Dylan Rogers's partner. They needed the man to give up the Coyote's true identity. They needed the exact location of the planned border breach, and they needed the day.

The drive to the jail was long and hot, the visit a complete bust. The truck driver had hanged himself in his cell just minutes before Mo had gotten there. He called in the news to the office.

They'd had nothing but bad luck on this mission so far. Too much bad luck. The enemy always seemed one step ahead. His instincts prickled. There was something here they weren't seeing. Maybe Sheriff Shane *was* involved. It sure seemed as if the bad guys were getting some help from somewhere. Except, Ryder had looked into Sheriff Shane, and the man had come up squeaky clean. He thought about that as he headed off to the hotel to pick up Molly and Logan.

He wanted to greet her with a kiss, but couldn't in front of her son. How they handled that would have to be her decision.

"Did you find everything okay?" he asked as they were headed down in the elevator.

"Yes, thank you. And I want you to know that we will pay you back for everything."

There was a coolness to her tone that he hadn't heard since the first time he'd met her, when he'd been interrogating her. He winced at the memory.

"That's not necessary."

"Yes, it is."

The elevator stopped and Logan darted out. Mo tried to take her hand, but she pulled away.

Okay. What was that about?

He didn't get the chance to ask on the ride out to her place. And they didn't have much privacy while taking care of the evening chores, either, with Logan always within hearing distance.

He gave up trying, and while she did the milking, a chore that proved him a complete klutz and no help whatsoever, he took Logan to the backyard for some extra self-defense training.

"Hey, Mo, watch this!" Logan executed a pretty good punch to his solar plexus.

"Not that hard, remember? You want to show them that you can defend yourself. The goal is to prevent a real fight, so nobody gets hurt."

"What if somebody punches me hard?"

"You fight back just enough to make them stop. You won't respond blindly. You gain control of the situation."

The kid nodded solemnly.

"You can train with me as hard as you like. But only with me, okay?" Now that the kid would be cooped up in the apartment all day instead of running around the ranch, he needed a little extra exercise.

"So what do you do when someone tries to grab you from the front?" Mo stepped forward and reached out.

Logan deflected.

"What if they grab you by the foot?"

They kept on training. And he thought of his talk with Ryder, how being connected to them could put Molly and Logan in more danger. He would make sure that didn't happen. But being prepared was the key.

"What if they have a weapon?"

Logan's eyes went round. "I'm in elementary school."

"Right. I meant like a stick or something." He showed the kid a twist kick, just the right place to hit the wrist to send a weapon flying.

And then he turned and caught Molly watching.

"You shouldn't take up so much of Mo's time," she told her son. And then to Mo, "I'm done. We're ready to leave."

Logan talked about some of the games he'd been playing on the console, all the way home. Molly barely said anything. She looked almost relieved when Mo left them at the hotel. The only thing she told him was to make sure he ate something from her fridge and didn't go hungry.

Why did women have to be like that? Did they know how much they confused men? Did they do it on purpose?

He drove back to the ranch and pulled up the driveway. He missed the dogs running to greet him. He got out of the car and walked around, checked the buildings to make sure nobody had come by while he'd been gone.

Nelly gave him her evil look as he walked through the barn.

"Don't think I'm going to go close enough for a kick. I've taken enough abuse already in this barn." He could swear the cow grinned at him.

Mo looked in on the horses next. Paulie, the half-blind gelding, turned his good eye toward him and gave him a mournful expression.

"You're not fooling me, buddy. I know you're just milking this for everything it's worth." But he had an apple for the horse, and for Sid and Gypsy, too, and one for Kenny Davis's Charlie.

He closed everything up behind him, then walked up to the house, went in with the key Molly had given him. Didn't look as if anyone had been in there or tried to get in.

He opened the fridge for some tea. The leftover lasagna on the top shelf looked like heaven. *Later.*

He drank then went back outside. A couple of things about last night bothered him. The Taser for one. Not standard smuggler ammo. The people who smuggled contraband across the border were usually armed with more serious weapons and wouldn't hesitate to shoot anyone, even each other, right in the face at the slightest sign of trouble.

So what was up with the Taser here?

He hoped the bastards would come back. Of course, now they knew that Molly wasn't entirely defenseless and alone out here, they would be more careful. Not that they hadn't been careful last night.

They'd come after the lights in the house were turned off. After Mo's pickup had disappeared from the driveway.

Which meant they probably kept an eye on the place. Probably drove by a few times first, checked things out.

He sat in the deepest shadows of the porch, the scent of her yellow roses all around him, and watched the cars on the road. Traffic was sparse this time of the night. None of the cars that passed the house slowed. From where he was sitting, he had no way of telling whether any of the drivers were checking out her place.

He got his SUV out of the garage and drove to the end of the road then set up a one-man roadblock. Ten minutes passed before the first pickup rolled along. Mo stuck a CBP badge on his shirt, flagged the car down with his flashlight and asked for license and registration.

"Anything wrong?" the seventysomething man asked, pushing back his cowboy hat, his face leathered with old age. He squinted from the flashlight as Mo scanned the cab.

"Standard vehicle check. We've had some extra activity in the past week. More illegal shipments than we normally see." Mo handed the papers back, making sure to remember the name. In the morning, he would run everyone through the system back at the office, see if anything popped up.

"Good luck," the man said and drove away.

Mo checked the next car and the next. A pickup had two rifles on the gun rack in the back, but just regular hunting rifles. Almost everyone had at least one of those around here. No Tasers in sight and no serious firearms, either, nothing that would be used by professional smugglers.

Midnight passed by the time the first car rolled by that seemed out of place—a fancy SUV, close to the hundred-grand price tag. Mexican license plates. An Asian guy sat behind the wheel. He almost didn't stop, but at the last moment seemed to decide not to drive around Mo. A very lucky decision on his part, since Mo wasn't in the best of moods by that point.

He was tired and getting hungry. And frustrated because his mind kept returning to Molly and he had no idea why she was giving him the cold shoulder. And doubly frustrated because he was getting nothing out of the roadblock, dammit, nothing that looked suspicious or seemed like any kind of a lead.

"License and registration," he said as he stepped up to the driver's side window.

"I left my wallet at hotel." The man frowned. "What is this? I'm in a hurry. I have business meetings in morning."

Mo looked him over dispassionately, not the least impressed by the fancy car, fancy suit and tone of superiority. He panned the inside of the car with his flashlight. "You have no ID?"

"I'm Yo Tee. You call mayor about me. He tell you who I am."

Mo glanced at his watch—almost one in the morning. "I don't think we'll be calling the mayor. Why don't you get out of the car, sir."

"I have no time. I am important person. Everyone know who I am." He reached for the shift to put the car in Drive.

Mo reached inside and clamped his wrist. "I wouldn't try that."

He opened the door and pulled the guy out, pushed him against the vehicle and patted him down as he protested and yelled about racial profiling.

He wasn't carrying a weapon, but Mo did notice a pretty fancy semiautomatic in a holster behind the passenger seat, which he'd missed earlier because it was blocked by the door frame. Since the weapon was now in plain sight, it was fair game.

"I own factory in Mexico. You make big mistake." The

man swore at him first in Chinese and then in Spanish as Mo cuffed him and put him in the back of his SUV.

Then he called Jamie. "I got someone here. Armed, without papers. Money to burn from the looks of it."

The region was pretty hard hit by the economic downturn. Not many people ran around in cars like his. Some of the ones who did made their fortunes in illegal smuggling.

"He claims to be some big-time businessman."

"Legal or illegal?"

"Exactly. I wouldn't mind having prints run through the system, if you could come get him."

"On my way."

While he waited for Jamie, he pulled over another couple of cars. He hit pay dirt when he shone his flashlight into a beaten-up green pickup.

The driver handed over his papers with his left hand, then turned his swarthy face from the light, his right hand in his lap.

His driver's license said Garcia Cruz. Same name as the guy killed with the knife that had slashed Molly's tires. Then again, there had to be probably a hundred Garcia Cruzes in the state. It was a common name. Still…

"Hands on the steering wheel where I can see them." Mo didn't want him to try to go for a weapon.

The guy put his hands up, trying to cover one with the other.

What was he trying to hide?

Mo went for his gun. "Step out of the vehicle, sir."

And then, as the man did, Mo saw the bandages.

"What happened to your hand?"

The man shrugged, looking at his feet. He wore scuffed work boots, dirty jeans and a sweaty muscle shirt. "Fingers got cut in the reaper."

"How many?"

"Three."

A man who just happened to be missing three fingers. What were the chances? They'd need a DNA test to match him up to the fingers found on the border, but Mo was pretty sure they'd found their guy. That put him in a much better mood.

By the time Jamie got there, he was damn near smiling. Progress was a beautiful thing.

Jamie took in Garcia and Yo Tee, who was still yelling for his cell phone and his lawyer. Mo stayed the whole night, stopped every car that went through. They were mostly locals, but he did catch two illegal border crossers, teens, with nearly forty pounds of weed. Looked like an amateur operation, small-time fish swimming way below the notice of the big-time smugglers.

Jamie came for the entrepreneurial teens, too. Everyone who was taken in would get printed, questioned, then turned over to Customs and Border Protection when Mo's team was done with them.

Keith called him at seven, just as he'd headed inside Molly's house to get some coffee and breakfast. He was pretty much starving by that point. Molly's lasagna tasted even better than it looked. Not being the type to cut corners, she packed all the wholesome goodness into it that she could.

The house seemed empty without her. The ranch missed her. Oh, hell, *he* missed her. He had to figure out why she was mad at him.

"Just got back," Keith was saying. "Got nothing. Everyone's sitting tight. Want me to go out to the ranch and stay with the Rogers woman while she does her thing? I can do that before I turn in."

"I'm out here already. Thanks." He needed to go back

to his place for a shower and a clean set of clothes. Might as well bring Molly back with him.

He finished his breakfast, locked up, then drove into Hullett.

He ran into her in the lobby.

"Where's Logan?"

"I just put him on the school bus." Her smile was strained. "It's a different bus for him. Different driver. Different students. That's a big deal for kids."

"Was he nervous?"

She looked away. "I was. He thought it was great to be picked up at a fancy hotel. And he couldn't wait to tell the other kids about your gaming setup."

They went up in the elevator together. She smelled like his shampoo. He wanted to pull her closer, but she definitely kept her distance.

"Long night?" she asked as they got off on the top floor. "Any trouble?"

"I don't mind trouble."

She stared at him as if he was crazy.

"Looking for trouble is my job, kind of."

She nodded. "I'll be out at the ranch for a while. You can have your place to yourself to get some rest."

"I'll just shower and change," he said. "I'll take you back and stick around while you finish up."

For a second she looked as if she would protest, but then she simply nodded and thanked him.

By the time he'd showered—trying hard not to think that she had been in his shower already this morning, naked—she had breakfast ready for him in the kitchen. And he found he was hungry again. Hey, how often did he have someone cook for him?

Might as well take advantage of it while he could. He pretty much inhaled the bacon and eggs, slowed down for the pancakes that were covered in something red and gooey and tasted like heaven.

"What's that?"

She looked up from the counter, where she was writing something in a notebook. "Prickly pear jelly. I make a few dozen jars every year. I brought some over. Logan likes it."

He licked his lips. "I appreciate this. Best breakfast I've had in a long time." Then he added, "The lasagna was great, too." He could definitely get used to eating like that on a regular basis.

He went around her to rinse his plate and put it in the dishwasher, turned around just as she turned back to reach for something. He knocked her off balance and wrapped her in his arms so she wouldn't be knocked against the counter. "Sorry."

Their gazes locked.

Under the scent of the soap, he could smell her soft skin.

He'd wanted her from the moment he'd first seen her, and had spent half of last night thinking about her.

He wanted to taste her lips so badly he thought he'd go cross-eyed from desire. He needed to romance her. That was what women wanted, wasn't it? He knew he should say something, compliment her on her hair or her clothes or whatever.

"Listen, I—" But then he just pressed his lips against hers.

This time, the wave of blinding need didn't catch him by surprise as it had at their first kiss. This time he knew what to expect, and yet the sensation still nearly knocked him off his feet.

They had some instant chemistry that made him want to pick her up and carry her off to his bed like a caveman. As bad as he was around women, even he knew that wasn't acceptable. Women needed courting. And sweet words.

Romance, he thought again. The very word struck fear into the heart of most every man. God help him.

So he kept on kissing her before she could start missing any of that.

"This is not wrong," he said when they came up for air.

His body grew hard. He didn't want to scare her, so he tried to move back a little. Instead, he somehow ended up pushing her against the counter.

SHE HAD ABOUT as much brain as a weather vane. She'd done this before, allowed herself to become a rich man's plaything. It had ended badly. "Yes, it is." And yet she couldn't make herself push Mo away when he leaned in for another kiss.

The first words out of his mouth when he'd come through the door downstairs had been to ask after her son. He always did that. And each time he did, it melted a little bit of her heart.

He was probably faking interest in her and her son just to get into her pants. Other men had done that before. She was such a terrible judge of men, just really bad at making big decisions altogether.

If she were smart, she would run right now.

Instead, she let him lift her up onto the counter.

Instead of protesting, she opened her knees so he could get closer. His hardness pressed against her, and she reveled in his thorough kiss, in his obvious need for her.

Heaven knew she wanted him. He woke up every one of her dormant desires.

Stop. You can still stop. Stop now, a small voice of sanity said in her head.

He ran his fingers up her arms, his touch on her naked skin sending delicious shivers through her. Heat grew inside and flooded her body. Need pulsed in her blood.

"Beautiful," he whispered as he trailed kisses down her neck.

She felt safe with him. She really, really liked him—the way he was nice to Logan, that he cared about her safety and her animals, down to the last scrawny chicken.

The temptation to fall headfirst into something here was overpowering. But as her eyes fluttered half-open, her gaze caught on the granite countertop and the ten-thousand-dollar stove.

And she couldn't ignore the stark truth, that she didn't belong in this place, with this man.

She pulled back. "I shouldn't be doing this. None of this is real."

"Why?"

"Because life is unfair. Why couldn't you be a plain cowboy? Why do you have to be a millionaire playboy G.I. Joe or whatever you are?" She held up a hand. "Please don't protest. You and your team are definitely not some desk-jockey administrators."

A smile hovered over his sexy lips. "Millionaire playboy G.I. Joe?"

"Seriously, how many of those are running around in the average Texas small town? And I have to hook up with one? I don't have to do this just because I like it so much. I like chocolate, too, and I don't eat it for breakfast, lunch and dinner"

"So you like it?"

"More than chocolate," she said on a sigh.

He grinned and brushed his lips over hers again, and she lost all ability to protest.

Her luck was nothing if not rotten.

Even if right now, this part seemed okay. Better than okay. Pretty good. *Great*.

He cupped the back of her neck with one hand and her

breast with the other as he deepened the kiss. Pleasure shot through her, straight to her toes. She'd gone without passion for so long. What was wrong with taking a little of this? Just once?

After an eternity, he pulled back, banked fires burning in his gaze. "I didn't plan this."

"I know. It's okay." She closed the distance between their lips. She needed just one more kiss.

She expected nothing from him, was fully aware that this could go no further. She would be his temporary entertainment. As long as she kept that fixed firmly in her head, she would be okay.

She was no starry-eyed schoolgirl. She no longer believed in happily ever after. When Mo walked away, she wouldn't be heartbroken like before. And she wouldn't be left pregnant. He had to have a maxi-pack of condoms somewhere in this apartment. He was rich and sexy. He probably had women in his life who were classy and sophisticated.

And they probably had lots of fabulous, even scandalous, sex, things she didn't even know how to do. Self-doubt tore into her suddenly. Because she was just a country bumpkin pretty much. She had to face it.

And that was as far as she got with thinking.

His thumb flicked over her nipple and it drew into a tight bud. Moisture gathered between her legs.

She gave up trying to form coherent thoughts and gave herself over to the pleasure of being seduced by Moses Mann. If he thought she was hopelessly unsophisticated and inexperienced, let that be his problem.

He reached for the top button on her shirt. Fumbled. Ha!

She found it incredibly flattering that he was as affected as she. That he wanted her so badly his fingers trembled.

Her knees were so week, if she was standing, she would have probably folded.

The top button yielded at last.

Then the next.

His warm, seeking lips moved down her neck, leaving a tingling trail of desire.

She shrugged out of the shirt before he was half-done with the buttons. He gave an appreciative sound in the back of his throat as he took in her simple cotton bra.

Then he looked pained. "I don't know what to say."

Who wanted to talk? She reached to the back to unclasp the bra. Heat flared in his eyes. He put his hands on her and drew the flimsy material away inch by inch, revealing her breasts with agonizing slowness.

"I want—" he started, but then just dipped his head and drew a nipple between his lips.

As pleasure spiraled through her, for a second she thought she was going to go over the edge right then and there.

Modest country girl, mother and all that.

Having sex in a fancy hotel, on the kitchen counter!

She was wicked, wicked, wicked.

He took her other nipple, drew on it gently, and her body shivered in delight. A strangled sound escaped her throat, halfway between a sob and a moan.

He pulled back. "Did I hurt you?"

She couldn't answer. She just shook her head.

"I want you." He held her gaze. "I wish I knew some romantic way to say that."

He looked concerned, as if he was afraid that what he did say wouldn't be enough.

She felt a smile stretch her lips. "I like plain and honest. I'm not exactly a big-time player."

"I want to pick you up and carry you back to the bedroom."

She slid an inch forward.

His lips tightened. "I don't have protection. I don't suppose you're…"

She stared at him. The millionaire playboy G.I. Joe didn't have protection?

She could have cried as she shook her head. Her entire body ached to finish what they had started. A few long seconds passed before the haze cleared from her mind.

And then she drew her shirt closed and took a deep breath.

Maybe tomorrow she'd be happy that nothing happened between them, but right now, she was awash in disappointment. She tried to remind herself that they weren't in the same league. That he was just playing here.

"Probably for the best," she forced herself to say. She avoided his gaze as she slid off the counter. "My animals are waiting. I usually feed them pretty early."

He let her go. "I need to grab something from the bedroom." His voice sounded a little rough as he said the words.

She straightened her clothing as he walked away. Then, needing something to do, she went back to her notebook and stuffed it into her purse.

Mo was coming back already. "What's that?"

She glanced at the notebook that stuck out of her bag. "I'm making a list of the people I'll need to contact to get Dylan's name cleared. I want something publicly said. In the paper."

"Molly—"

"No." She held up a hand. She didn't want him to say anything bad about her brother right now. She couldn't handle it, not after what they'd just shared, what they had almost done.

Something they shouldn't have done, really. It wasn't as if they were a couple or anything, or as if he even believed her about Dylan.

"Can we—" She glanced toward the counter. "Could we please just forget that this happened?"

His answer was a long time coming. But then he said, "Sure."

She didn't dare look up into his face.

The elevator ride down was awkward, the car ride to the ranch spent in silence. She ran from him the second she slipped out of the car, keeping away from him as she did her chores, pretty much the way she had the night before.

He knew what needed to be done at this stage, so he helped without asking anything, without following her, for which she was grateful. She needed time to recover.

When they were done, she went inside to clean up and water her plants. He was waiting for her in his car when she came out.

She slid into the passenger seat. "Thank you for bringing me here."

"We're doing everything we can to figure out what's going on so you can return home," he said, back in his official persona, his tone impersonal.

He drove down the driveway and turned right instead of turning left, toward Hullett. Maybe he wanted to drive around her land. She wasn't about to complain. It wasn't as if she needed to be anywhere in a hurry.

She leaned back in her seat, more than a little sleepy. She'd had a restless night. As luxurious as her room was, she wasn't used to sleeping in a strange bed.

She was up half the night, walking around. And once

she stopped being blinded by all that opulence, she realized how sterile it all seemed. Just a hotel suite, really.

Not one personal item graced the living room, nothing that said warmth or family. No pictures, no memories, no favorite mug with #1 Uncle on it or anything like that. Everything was decorated in just the standard white the hotel provided. All the luxuries didn't make the place a home. In some sense, she had so much more out at the ranch than he had in his big fancy hotel.

She was so lost in her thoughts she wasn't paying any attention to where he was driving, so she was surprised when they pulled over in front of an old cabin. "Where are we?"

But he was already getting out.

She followed him to the cabin and then inside. "What's this?"

"We're on the Cordero ranch. This is the cabin where Dylan shot and killed four of his accomplices."

Denial sprung to her lips, but died there as she spotted the rust-colored stains on the floor—blood that had seeped into the floorboards. Her stomach rolled. One by one, she noticed the holes where bullets had been pried out of the logs, probably by Mo's team.

"It can't—" Her voice broke.

"It happened. You need to somehow be able to accept that."

"You don't know—"

"I was here. I helped clean up the bodies."

"You were only here after," she whispered. "You don't know what happened."

"Grace Cordero was here during the shooting. Are you saying she's an unreliable witness?"

Grace.

The truth came crashing down on her so hard she couldn't breathe. The carnage here…the bloodbath…and

Grace had been in the middle of it. She could have been killed.

Molly turned and ran outside, ran behind Mo's car then fell to her knees and gave back her breakfast.

She heard his car door open and close, then he was there, gently helping her up, handing her a bottle of water.

"Just because Dylan did something bad here, it doesn't reflect on you or Logan," he said.

She couldn't talk. She rinsed her mouth, then walked to the passenger side and got in. She felt as if she'd just eaten poison.

He took his seat, too, and watched her with concern. "I'm sorry. I shouldn't have brought you here."

"No." She closed her eyes and leaned her head against the headrest, couldn't bear looking at the cabin. "The truth is always good, even if it hurts."

He started the car and drove away.

Minutes passed before she could open her eyes. She still couldn't look at him. She was so hurt and so ashamed.

Oh, Dylan, what have you done?

How had she not known that her brother had gotten involved in smuggling? If they'd talked more, if she'd asked more questions…

"I can't tell Logan," she said at last, horror filling her at the thought. Logan would be devastated.

"Then don't."

"I don't want to lie to him, either. At some point he will have to face the truth, too." That was the right way to go, not her denial. Mo had been right to take her to the cabin, even if it was ripping her apart right now.

"He'll have to accept this, yes, but it doesn't have to happen when he's eight years old. You can give him some of the truth. I don't think details would be necessary at this stage."

She nodded, feeling numb. "What will he think? I don't want him to feel bad about himself because of this."

"Just keep telling him you love him." He paused. Cleared his throat. "When I first found out about being dumped by my parents…" He shook his head. "They tried to drown their own kid. What the hell kind of person does that? And those are my genes. I think I went into the armed forces right out of high school because I wanted to be under close supervision, in case somehow the 'evil' broke out."

She turned to stare at him. "There's nothing evil about you. You're not your parents."

He held on to the wheel with one hand and took her hand with the other, gave a gentle squeeze. "And you're not your brother. And neither is Logan."

She looked away. "I can't talk to you about this."

TEARS BRIMMED IN HER EYES, the first one spilling over, rolling down her face. He felt like a jerk. She needed comfort, but he had no idea how to give it to her, not when she didn't want anything to do with him at the moment.

Mo couldn't blame her. He'd brought her here. He'd brought her this pain. And yet, being pushed away both frustrated and hurt him.

His phone rang. He glanced at it. Jamie. He had to take the call.

"There's movement on the border. The rest of the team is there. I'm heading out right now. Multiple breaches at multiple points." He gave GPS coordinates.

"I'll be right there."

"Try to avoid Ryder. The Chinese guy you got the other night, Yo Tee, he's the real deal. Big-money business guy. Lawyers filed a complaint and everything. Ryder isn't happy. Way to go not bringing attention to the op."

"He looked suspicious."

"Everyone who comes within a mile of Molly Rogers seems suspicious to you these days."

Maybe Jamie was right. Maybe he was losing his objectivity. He wasn't sure there was anything he could do about it. Molly was becoming more and more important to him. "I'll see you in a bit," he said, then ended the call, not feeling like making explanations to Jamie.

"Just take me back to the ranch." Molly still wouldn't look at him.

"You're not going to hang out at your place alone." He turned the car and sped down the dirt road that led to the Cordero ranch.

He might not have been able to help Molly right now, but he knew who could. And he would make sure she was in good hands before he left her. He hoped Grace Cordero was home.

Chapter Nine

Tension tightened Molly's shoulders as Mo pulled up in front of Grace's place.

"I think you should talk to her," he said. "But it's your choice." He waited.

Then Skipper came running, and for a moment she forgot about everything else and jumped from the car, caught the dog up into her arms. The unconditional love and support felt incredibly good.

She scratched behind the dog's ear before giving her another big hug and a kiss.

The front door of the house creaked open.

"Hey." Grace stepped outside. "I was just about to call you. She can go home whenever you're ready."

"I have to go," Mo told them from behind the wheel. "Can you take Molly back to the hotel when she's ready?"

As soon as Grace nodded, he drove away, with one last look at Molly, conflicting emotions darkening his face.

Grace tilted her head. "What's going on? What hotel is he talking about?"

Molly stood, but kept her hand on the dog's head. "I'm... Logan and I are not at the ranch right now. We're in Hullett."

"Everything okay?"

She hesitated. She had so much to say. And she didn't know where to start.

"Why don't we go inside?" Grace suggested. "How about a cold drink?"

She was being nice, a good hostess, but there was a wariness in her tone. Molly couldn't blame her.

She followed Grace inside and sat at the kitchen table, hugged Skipper. The dog stuck to her like glue.

Twinkie, a stray cat Grace had rescued a few weeks back, sauntered in from the direction of the laundry room.

"I hope Skipper was okay with Twinkie and the kittens." Grace had adopted a boxful of barn kittens, too, from a nearby ranch when their mother had disappeared.

"Very gentle." Grace poured two glasses of lemonade then set the pitcher between them.

And then they were out of neutral topics of conversation.

Molly drew a deep breath. "We need to talk about Dylan."

Grace's face grew somber as she pulled back a little. She probably expected an argument.

Molly folded her hands on her lap, not sure how to start. "I'm sorry." She was, and it had to be said.

"You haven't done anything." Absolution came quickly and without hesitation.

Her eyes burned. "Mo took me out to the cabin." A tear spilled over. Pain filled her chest. "Dylan… I don't understand. How could he? He was a good brother. He really was. He loved Logan." Another tear broke loose. "How can he have had this monster inside him? How did I not know this?"

"None of it was your fault." Grace came around the table and folded her into a group hug with Skipper, who'd jumped up on Molly to lick her face, needing to be in the middle of everything, as usual.

Molly hugged them back as warmth spread inside her chest. "Can you ever forgive me? I'm so glad you didn't get hurt. I'm so sorry, Grace. We were like sisters back in high school."

"We're still sisters." Grace smiled as she returned to her chair.

Molly blew her nose and dried her face. "Sorry," she said again, unable to think of anything else to say. The vivid image of the blood-splattered cabin loomed large in her head. "You should have never had to go through something like that."

"You have nothing to apologize for. Mo shouldn't have taken you to the cabin. You really didn't need to see that place."

Protectiveness instead of blame. They'd been best friends once. Was it possible that the damage wasn't irreparable?

"He was right. I needed to face the truth. Denial is not healthy."

Grace nodded slowly. "How is Logan?"

"Getting into fights at school." She shook her head. "Mo is… He's teaching him how to stand up for himself, how to avoid violence and how to defend himself if he can't avoid it."

"So Mo is spending a lot of time with you two?" A glint of interest came into Grace's eyes. "He used to scare me. He's so big and rough-looking. But I'm pretty sure he's a gentle giant. He came to Tommy's funeral. All of Ryder's friends did."

"I'm sorry I didn't." The funeral had been right after Dylan's death when she'd been drowning in grief, blaming everyone around her.

"I shouldn't have brought that up. I didn't mean it as a

reproach." Grace winced. "You had a lot to deal with. We both lost brothers we love. I understand."

Except Grace had lost a brother who was a war hero, while Molly had lost a brother who was apparently the town villain. She pushed the bitterness back, determined not to let it get a toehold. "Yes," she agreed.

"I'm glad Mo is spending time with Logan. Whatever else Dylan did, he was a good uncle."

Tears burned Molly's eyes all over again. "Thank you for understanding that."

Grace tilted her head. "So what's this with Mo? I thought you were dating Kenny."

"Temporary insanity." She bit her lip. "We are kind of living at Mo's place."

A smile teased Grace's lips. "You want to tell me something?"

Definitely not that little incident on the kitchen counter. She felt herself flush. The way she'd just abandoned all sense... Not like her at all. Thank goodness she was sane now. Nothing like that was going to happen between her and Mo again.

"He's very helpful," she said.

Grace raised an eyebrow. "I'll bet." Then her mouth curved into a smile. "Have you seen the rest of his team?"

"Some of them."

She fanned herself with her hand. "Lord have mercy."

And then they giggled like two schoolgirls, just like back in the good old days, their friendship mending.

That mended link went a long way toward her feeling better, Molly thought on her way back to the hotel with Grace. Just the two of them. Grace agreed to keep Skipper a little longer. Three dogs in the presidential suite might have been a little too much for hotel management.

"I need to pick up something at the strip mall for Ryder's birthday," Grace said. "Do you mind if we stop in?"

Molly shook her head. She wasn't in a hurry. "What is he getting?"

"Lingerie." Grace grinned.

Molly grinned back. And then it was like two best friends out on the town, and it felt amazing.

So while Grace shopped, Molly picked up a personalized coffee mug made for Mo with his name on it and a super-muscled arm for the handle. MO COFFEE. She hoped he would get a kick out of that.

She picked him up a pretty country pitcher perfect for sweet tea. She bought ingredients so she could make a few dinners, and some plastic storage containers to freeze single portions so he could have some homemade food now and then. He seemed to enjoy her cooking. She was in the checkout line when she ran back and grabbed everything she needed to bake some cookies, as well.

She started cooking as soon as Grace dropped her off at the hotel. Then when Logan came home from school, they baked up a storm together.

Then waited for Mo.

But Mo never came.

THE BORDER OP was a bust—half a dozen people who were carrying nothing. They were first-timers, looking for work. They confessed as soon as they were apprehended. They'd been told to cross and were shown the right spot for free.

A test.

Whoever was running the smuggling rings wanted to know how closely the border was watched. They sent over some decoys, then probably watched from the other side of the river with binoculars as the decoys were caught.

Mo staked out the ranch again that night, actually slept

some on her sofa. He needed to catch up on rest or he'd start making mistakes. Like kissing her in the kitchen.

He'd gotten carried away. She was living at his place. When he'd offered his apartment, he'd meant it to be a sanctuary. She should be able to live there in peace, without being harassed by him because he couldn't control his lust.

But every time he saw her, he wanted her. So maybe the key was to stay away from her, at least for the time being.

Toward dawn he set up another roadblock. He stopped a couple of cowboys going to work early. They weren't thrilled with the harassment. He wasn't thrilled with his lack of progress. He needed a new plan.

He called Jamie. "I'm heading in. Can you drive out here and stick around while Molly takes care of her morning chores?"

Time to get out of here. Even if he did want to see her. Even if he wanted to do way more than just see her. Well, especially because of that.

SINCE THEY ALL DROVE the same model black SUV, Molly couldn't tell who'd be helping her today until Jamie walked out of the barn as she pulled into her driveway.

She'd been hoping for Mo, wondered why he hadn't come home last night.

"Is Mo okay?" The words flew from her mouth before she remembered her manners. "Good morning."

"Good morning. He's at the office. He was out here all night."

She wished he'd stuck around, but tried not to show her disappointment.

"Where are we starting today?" Jamie asked.

"I need to do the milking."

He nodded. "How about if I let out the chickens?"

He was a nice guy, handsome, mild, although that mildness hid plenty of restrained power. He didn't smile much, or ever, really. There were walls all around him that were nearly palpable. She wondered what had happened to him, but she didn't dare ask.

Instead, she headed off to get her buckets, then headed to the barn and greeted the cows.

She didn't mind being at Mo's place as much as she thought she would, and Logan treated it like a vacation, glued to the video games. He thought the whirlpool tub was great and the fancy electronics still made him go wide-eyed.

But Molly missed her house.

She did her chores and Jamie helped, although she insisted he shouldn't. He was supposed to be here to make sure she was safe. He could have sat in his air-conditioned car; he didn't need to be stepping in chicken droppings for her sake. But, of course, he wouldn't hear of it. Like Mo, he had an inner sense of honor and chivalry.

The cowboy code, some people around here called it. Except none of the men on Mo's team were cowboys, although some of them had adopted the local dress code of jeans and cowboy boots to fit in better.

Jamie pulled out of the driveway first, Molly right behind him, just stopping to get the mail out of the mailbox. She sat there, the car idling while she went through the stack of envelopes, hoping for no surprise bills. She had Dylan's mail, too, from the apartment, forwarded here, so she had a handful to go through.

Kenny's cruiser was coming down the road toward her place. Probably coming to check on his horse.

Jamie rolled his window down, his cell phone pressed to his ear. "Are we good here?"

"If you need to go someplace, go," she told him. "I'll be fine here with Kenny."

She set the organic-heirloom-seed catalogs on the passenger seat as Jamie pulled away. Then came a magazine on sustainable farming. Then a bunch of flyers. A credit-card solicitation. Then something that did look like a bill, from the Hullett Storage Park. She tore open the envelope. Huh. Dylan was renting some storage.

For what? They had plenty of room at the ranch for anything he would have needed to store.

Unless it was something he didn't want her to know about…

Her head snapped up and she reached for the horn, but Jamie had already disappeared down the road. She drew a deep breath. Might not be anything important, in any case.

Then she caught herself. She had to stop making excuses for Dylan. She had to accept that he was capable of doing wrong. She reached for her purse on the floor to call Mo, but by the time she dug her cell phone out from the bottom, Kenny's patrol car was pulling up next to her.

He didn't look like his usual spiffy self. His hair was mussed. Dark circles ringed his eyes. "Everything okay? I've been by a couple of times. Your pickup wasn't here."

Right. She'd forgotten to tell him. "Mo thought I shouldn't be out here alone with Logan at night. We're staying in Hullett."

His eyebrows slid up his forehead. "I thought Dylan's apartment wasn't released yet."

"Mo rents a place he doesn't really use. He let us have it."

"You're staying with Moses Mann?" Kenny's forehead pulled together into a scowl.

"Not with him. Just at his place. He only stops in for a change of clothes."

Kenny's lips flattened. "Isn't he a dedicated government employee?" He watched her for a second. "When are they gonna be done with their budget recommendations?"

"I'm not sure. He doesn't really talk about his job."

"Bunch of idiot pencil pushers flown in from D.C. Think they can drive around the border for a few weeks, have everything figured out. I've lived here all my life, worked here since I got my badge. You'd think CBP would be asking people like me if they needed help."

She wasn't sure what exactly Mo was, but she was pretty sure he wasn't a pencil pusher. The way he moved, the way he was built... All she could think of was the commando soldiers she'd seen in movies.

"They do work pretty hard," she said, defending the team. They put in some serious hours. They wanted to figure out what was going on at the border, and they gave the task their all. While taking time to protect her. "You look tired," she said to change the subject.

"Been pulling some double shifts." Kenny tilted his head. "So this Mo and his super team still blame your brother for everything?"

She closed her eyes for a second. "I— It looks like Dylan might have somehow gotten involved in something he shouldn't have." It hurt just saying the words.

"They know that for a fact?" Kenny leaned forward. "They have any idea who he might have been working with?"

"I don't know. I just..." She lifted the bill on her lap. "Got a bill for a storage unit he was renting in Hullett."

He stared at the envelope, an unreadable expression on his face. "Could be nothing." He reached a hand out the open window toward her. "Let me see it."

She handed the bill over and waited while Kenny scanned the contents then handed the envelope back to her.

"You shouldn't go out there. Don't put your fingerprints

on anything. Moses Mann and those yahoos are desperate to pin all their problems on someone. Make sure it's not you. You don't want them to take you in for another interrogation."

He was right about that. But she didn't think Mo's team were a bunch of yahoos. Still. "I'm not planning on going anywhere near that storage unit."

"If you want, I can go check it out after my shift is over tonight. Nobody has to know about it until then."

She nodded. "Thanks, Kenny."

"You'd probably do best if you stayed away from those outsiders. They think they're hotshots, know everything better, look down on us country folk. They're not like you and me, Molly."

That Kenny would think that didn't surprise her. Hullett and Pebble Creek were small towns, filled with people whose ancestors had lived on the borderlands for generations. They were fiercely proud of that and protective of their heritage. Newcomers were often greeted with suspicion. They usually came to take.

She exchanged a few more words with Kenny before parting ways. She wanted to deliver her vegetables before they completely wilted in the back.

She was almost in town when Mo called to check on her.

Kenny had said nobody had to know about the storage unit. But Mo...

"I just got a bill from the storage park in Hullett. It looks like Dylan was renting a unit," she told him on impulse, then wondered if she'd done the right thing.

MO HAD BEEN OUT by the border investigating a rope line across the river that had gone up overnight, either to help people cross or to pull contraband. He got in his car as soon as Molly told him about the storage unit, but it took him an hour to reach Hullett. The GPS led him straight to the storage park. He marched into the office, flashed his CBP badge and asked for the locker number assigned to Dylan Rogers.

"And I'll need a lock cutter, too. I'm sure you have one of those back there somewhere," he told the twentysomething clerk behind the desk who was covered in tattoos from head to toe.

"I don't know, dude. Do you have, like, a search warrant?" The kid chewed his wad of gum, patting his greasy goatee.

Mo had a Beretta in his holster, good enough for a padlock, he figured. He didn't have time to play here. "Never mind. Just point me to the locker."

The kid shook his head. "You can't just bust into somebody's locker, man."

To hell with him. Mo strode out of the office and straight into the maze of lockers, followed the signs and numbers until he reached 763. The clerk caught up with him, protesting.

Then gaped at the sight that greeted them.

The lock had been busted off the unit, the space empty save for some some packing peanuts scattered around on the floor.

Mo glanced up at the security camera. Broken. Chunks of plastic lay on the ground. Still, it might have caught something before it connected with a baseball bat or whatever.

"I'm going to need the security footage."

The kid backed away. "You're gonna need a search warrant, man."

He didn't have time for a search warrant. This was their best lead in weeks and it was fresh. He'd be damned if he was going to waste it. He looked the kid over, considered a bullet in his kneecap.

He'd been on plenty of missions where interrogations had been conducted like that. But he believed that senseless violence was never an intelligent man's first weapon. So he asked nicely. While pulling himself to full height and putting on his meanest face.

"How about I just look at the footage on your screen? I won't ask for the tape."

The clerk's Adam's apple bobbed up and down a few times. "Um...I suppose that would be okay."

But the tape proved to be no help whatsoever. It didn't show a damned thing. Whoever had taken out the camera had snuck up to it from behind. Since the unit was in the last row, near the employee entrance, no other cameras caught the guy, either. Looked as if he'd come in through the back. Mo was willing to bet that lock, too, would be busted.

The only clue he got was the time. The security footage stopped thirty minutes ago.

He thanked the clerk and called Molly on his way out. He needed to find out if she'd told anyone else about the storage bill.

But he couldn't reach her.

Chapter Ten

Molly tried not to think of the worst while she waited on the line to be transferred to the school office. The apartment was silent around her, the dogs sleeping in Logan's bedroom. Where Logan should have been right now, doing homework, but wasn't.

Maybe he'd gotten into another fight and was serving detention. That he hadn't come home on the school bus didn't have to mean anything worse than that.

She let out a pent-up sigh. They would definitely have to have another talk about fighting.

"Mrs. Langton," said the school secretary on the other end at last.

"Hi, this is Molly Rogers. Logan wasn't on the school bus. Could you please see what happened to him? Did he get detention?"

"Oh, are you okay?"

"Yes. Do you know where he is?"

"Sheriff Davis took him. Kenny said you were unavailable." An uncomfortable silence followed the last word.

"When?" Her phone beeped, an incoming call. She ignored it.

"Just as the buses were pulling out. Are you sure everything is okay? I thought—"

Mrs. Langton didn't have to finish. Molly knew what

she thought. That Molly had been arrested in connection with her brother's crimes, that Kenny was taking Logan to Social Services.

"Thanks. I'm sure it's just a misunderstanding." She hung up, confused and worried. She glanced at the phone. Mo had called. She was about to call him back and beg for his help when another call came in: Kenny.

"Why did you take Logan?"

"I haven't been completely honest with you, honey." A pause followed the words, then, "Your brother and I were kind of business partners. He took delivery of a considerable amount of merchandise. Then he died before we could have passed on the goods. Well, I thought he had, but as it turns out he hadn't. The people on the other side of the border want their money."

A sense of betrayal washed over her, sending a chill down her spine. She couldn't have cared less about money or merchandise or any of that stupid business. "Where is Logan?"

"Logan will be safe as long as you cooperate. I've been given an ultimatum over here, you understand. I would have rather done this the nice way. I had plans for you and me. But time is running out."

Her heart gave a long, hard squeeze. "What do you want?"

"The drugs. Looks like Dylan only used the storage locker as a temporary place. Or maybe he ran his distribution from there. There was nothing in it. I have twenty-four hours to come up with the full shipment. I'd rather not find out what will happen if I can't produce the goods. So it's the boy for the drugs. That's how simple it is. Nothing to worry about. You give me what I want, and the boy comes home."

Was he nuts? Cold fear spread through her, desperation constricting her throat. "I have no idea where any drugs are."

"You probably just don't know that you know. Nobody knew Dylan half as well as you did. I'm sure there's some clue in that house or in that pretty little head of yours that will lead us to the rest. You just have to want to find it. Twenty-four hours."

She was so upset, she couldn't talk.

"I'll be calling. And, in the meanwhile, I wouldn't tell anyone about this, especially your devoted friend, Moses Mann, and his team, if you know what's good for your kid," Kenny added. "If you tell anyone, I'll know it. If you want the kid back, the most important thing you can do is to keep this between us, honey."

SHE WASN'T AT THE HOTEL.

The dogs were happy to see him, though, jumping all over Mo as he strode in.

"Where is everybody?"

Max and Cocoa licked his face, but that was it. No information was forthcoming.

He looked through the apartment carefully, checking for any signs of forced entry or struggle. Everything seemed in its place.

Maybe Molly took Logan shopping. Although, it looked as if she'd already shopped. He noted the soft blanket folded over the back of the couch and the throw pillow that would make taking a nap there actually comfortable. He went for a drink and saw the sweet tea in a brand-new pitcher.

Okay, his place did lack the niceties. He mostly came here to sleep. She was making herself more comfortable, he thought, then noticed the coffee mug. MO COFFEE. And a dog-shaped cookie jar on the counter. He opened it and smiled. Cookies.

Warmth spread through him as he realized that she was trying to make life nicer for him.

And she had. Just her presence in his apartment had somehow transformed it. Molly and Logan made the place a home instead of a hotel suite.

He pulled out his phone and dialed her again. He'd tried several times already, but she wasn't picking up. This time the robot voice said the number was unavailable. Her phone was either turned off or her battery was dead.

Was she avoiding him again?

Too bad. He had to talk to her. He needed to know who else she told about the storage locker.

He called Jamie. "Was everything okay with Molly when you were out at the ranch with her this morning?"

"Fine. Why?"

"She's not at the hotel, and I can't reach her on the phone."

"I had to run off to follow up on a lead, but we were done by then, leaving. The Pebble Creek sheriff was coming to see his horse."

"Okay. I'll go out there. Maybe she went out early for the evening feeding." She really shouldn't have done that. She knew it wasn't safe.

He hung up then checked his weapons and hurried down to his car, pretty much ignoring the speed limit as he drove through town. He didn't relax until he was turning down her road and could see her pickup sitting in the driveway.

When he walked into the house, she was just coming down the stairs, her chestnut hair tied up in a haphazard bun. A dust streak stretched across her face. Looked as if she'd been cleaning.

"You shouldn't be here alone." Relief and frustration shot through him in a tangled mix. "You're going to risk your life for dust bunnies?"

"I've really been neglecting the place," she said apologetically without meeting his eyes.

"You still should have waited for me." He drew a slow breath. He hadn't come here to yell at her.

She gave a strained smile, the house silent around them. Too silent.

He looked around. "Where's Logan?"

She turned from him, her hands fidgeting over things as she tidied up the kitchen, her movements stiff and jerky. "He's at a friend's house."

"Everything okay?"

She nodded without turning around. "Just tired. I never sleep well in a strange place."

She wanted to come home. Of course. Thing was, he'd gotten used to her and Logan being there when he popped in for this and that. He liked it.

"Thanks for the mug," he said. "And all the rest, too." For the first time, the apartment actually looked lived-in. There were books and toys lying about. He wished he had the right words to tell her how he felt about that, how he felt about having her and Logan in his life. Instead, he turned to business. "I called you earlier."

"My battery is probably dead. I'll charge it when we get back to the hotel." She stood at the sink with her back to him.

"I need to ask you something. Have you told anyone else about the storage locker?"

Her shoulders tensed even more. "No." She didn't turn to face him. "I should go take care of the animals. After I finish up outside, I'll need to come back in here and gather up some things. You can leave if you have to go back to work. I should be okay."

Was she mad at him? It was as if she couldn't even stand

to look at him. But if she were mad, then what were the cookies and the mug and all the other stuff about?

God, women were confusing.

Maybe all those things were her way of paying him back for their stay. She didn't want to be beholden to him or some such nonsense. Completely unnecessary. He would have given her whatever she asked, everything he had.

Or maybe the cookies and all were Logan's idea. He loved the apartment and the game console.

"I'll walk around the outbuildings, see if I can find any tire tracks or some sign that people have been out here lately."

She nodded as she put something in the fridge.

It was plain that she wanted him gone.

So he obliged her by walking away.

MOLLY RUSHED BACK upstairs to Dylan's room as soon as Mo went outside. She needed to stay away from him. She'd almost told him about Logan a half-dozen times. But if Kenny found out she told… Kenny was a sheriff. He was listening to all the law-enforcement channels. He would know the second Mo passed the news on to his team.

Kenny… Oh, God. She searched through Dylan's dresser frantically, looking at every piece of paper in the bottom drawer. Most turned out to be old receipts for farm equipment, warranties and catalogs. She shoved the drawer shut, desperation washing over her as she stood.

There had been nothing in Dylan's desk, nothing under his mattress, either. Where else would he hide something? Of course, she had no idea what she was looking for. Receipts for another storage unit?

She went downstairs for the largest knife she had, then back up to test the floorboards to see if there might be some hidden nook where her brother had kept information.

One board did come up, and as it did, a spring shot off a rubber band that smacked her in the nose. One of Dylan's early booby traps. She looked at the empty vodka bottle in the hole as she rubbed her nose. Probably left over from Dylan's teenage years.

Where were the damn drugs?

How could Dylan get involved in something like this? How could Kenny? Kenny was a sheriff, for heaven's sake. He should have been on the side of good, steering her brother right, not dragging him into dirty business.

She couldn't trust anyone.

Her brother hadn't been who she thought he was. Kenny, a sheriff, had his own share of secrets. She wanted to trust Mo, she really did. But her judgment was so obviously terrible.

What if Mo, too, had his own secret agenda?

Maybe he'd only offered her the apartment to keep a closer eye on her. Maybe he didn't care about her one bit, only cared about his mission. He'd said as much before.

If she told him about Logan, would he and his team charge ahead to catch Kenny, not caring what happened to her son? Would they think one little kid was an acceptable casualty when they had border security at risk?

She desperately needed a friend in all this, but there was too much at stake. She couldn't talk to anyone, not even Grace. Grace could tell Ryder.

She gave up on Dylan's room and went through all the others, feeling more desperate and more alone than she'd ever felt in her life. She knew only one thing: she would do anything to save her son. She would sacrifice anything. If she found any drugs, or any indication of where they were hidden, she would hand them over to Kenny in the blink of an eye. Even if it meant she had to go to prison afterward.

But she found nothing.

She went back down to the kitchen and happened to glance at the answering machine. The light was blinking. She hadn't seen that earlier. She had four messages, three from telemarketers, one from the agent for Brandsom Mining. She deleted them all.

Even if she eventually got desperate enough to call Brandsom, she had the agent's card. He'd sent it in the mail, along with various offers. Several times.

The thought that things might come to that further twisted her heart. Dylan had always been very adamant about not letting anyone near the old mine shafts.

She froze where she stood.

The old mine shafts.

Some had collapsed, while others had been blown in on purpose to make sure local teens didn't go in there to do whatever teens did when they were hiding from their parents. The shafts were way too dangerous. All the openings had been boarded up. But what if…

If there was a spot on the ranch where multiple crates of something could be hidden, those old mine shafts would be it.

She looked outside, into the approaching darkness. She had only a vague idea where the openings were. She would never find them in the dark. She'd be lucky to find them in the daylight.

The thought that she would have to wait brought tears of frustration into her eyes. She wanted her son back and she wanted him now. She blinked away the tears. She couldn't afford to break down. Best thing was to keep busy.

She went outside and hurried through her chores, trying her best to avoid Mo as much as possible. She didn't want him to realize that she was upset. She didn't want to chance him guessing that something was wrong.

He was cleaning off his boots when she finished up and came out of the barn, closing it up behind her for the night.

"Thank you." She did her best to put on a smile. "You probably have to go back to work. I'm going to head over to Grace's place for a little while."

But he said, "I don't think Grace is home. She was going to help Ryder with something tonight."

"Oh. Well." She tried not to look as frustrated as she felt. "I suppose I'll go to the feed store, then." She waited for him to leave.

"I'll go with you."

Great. "I shouldn't take up all your time."

"I don't mind. I have the night off."

And true to his word, he stuck by her. So she was forced to go to the feed store, pick up things she didn't really need, drop them off at the barn, then head back to Hullett with him.

All the while worrying about her son, petrified that she wouldn't be able to save him.

"WHEN IS LOGAN coming home?" Mo asked over dinner. He was glad he'd taken the night off. Something was wrong with Molly. He needed to figure out what.

"Tomorrow," she said ashen-faced without looking up from her plate.

The dogs lay at her feet. They didn't beg for food. They were pretty well behaved.

"It's good that he has close friends. He's a pretty special little kid. You raised him well."

She ate, but without true appreciation. Were her eyes glistening?

Looked as if all the stress was really getting to her. He felt guilty as hell. She'd lost her brother, her only support, had some financial issues at the ranch, was accused of being involved in smuggling and had been interrogated. And then he'd taken her to that damn cabin.

Which might not have been the best decision he'd ever made. She clearly needed something to hang on to, and some false ideal of Dylan had been it. Now that he'd taken that away from her, she had nothing.

He was wired differently. He needed the truth. He would take any truth, no matter how harsh, and then he could deal with it. He liked to know where he stood. He didn't believe in clinging to fantasies.

"You're a strong woman. You will work through this," he told her, reaching for her hand across the table.

She pulled away. "I'm not strong. Not like you are," she said miserably.

"You might not be jumping in front of bullets on a daily basis, but what you do day after day, running the ranch, raising your son, takes strength."

The sight of a tear rolling down her face twisted his gut.

"Hey." He reached across the table again and brushed away the tear with his thumb.

She pushed her seat back so fast she nearly knocked it over. "Better get started on the dishes."

He stood. "I'll do that."

But she was already standing by the sink.

"How about you wash, I dry," he said, offering a compromise. She accepted.

They worked in silence for a while, their movements strangely harmonized as if they'd done this often. She looked at him a couple of times, as if on the verge of saying something, but each time she changed her mind and turned away.

"How about some TV?" he suggested when they were done. She looked as if she could use some distraction.

She looked toward her bedroom, then nodded. "Sure."

He flipped through the channels, found a sappy romantic comedy. Supposedly women liked that kind of thing. He tried to think what else he could do to cheer her up. Flowers. Women usually found flowers comforting. He glanced around the apartment. She'd brought him some sort of potted herb. The pot stood behind them on the sofa table. He put his arm over the back of the sofa as unobtrusively as he could and pushed the plant closer to her.

She looked up at him, a moment of confusion on her face.

Right. Because it looked as if he had his arm up there to kind of drop it over her shoulders. As if he was making a move.

He acted as though he was just stretching, then pulled back and stared straight ahead at the TV, where a pair of rambunctious dogs were wrapping their owners together with their leashes.

Max padded in, barked at the screen, then, after Molly patted him, he went back out to the kitchen. He liked lying on the tile floor. It was probably colder.

The movie went on. Minutes ticked by.

She looked straight ahead, but he wasn't sure she was really watching. Her shoulders were still tight, the look on her face still unhappy.

He hated that he couldn't help her, watched the movie without registering much of it, thinking mostly about Molly beside him. Truth was, he wanted to pull her into his arms and distract her from her troubles in the most ancient way. By making love to her.

He wasn't proud of himself for the thought. What kind of man would use a woman's temporary distress to seduce her?

In the movie, the heroine was going through her troubles alone, consoling herself with copious amounts of ice cream.

He wished he had some of that in the freezer. Or chocolate. He tried to think what he had in his half-empty cabinets. Then cheered up a little when he thought of something.

"How about some beef jerky?"

She drew her eyebrows together. "Are you hungry? We just ate."

"I meant for..." He almost said *female upset* but finished lamely with "dessert."

A dubious look flashed across her face. "We have cookies," she reminded him. "Maybe later. But thank you," she said politely, then went back to watching the movie.

He tried to think of something that might work to relax her. Maybe a bubble bath. Women liked that, didn't they?

The image of her naked in his tub resulted in a predictable response from his body. He shifted in his seat. But his condition only worsened when the star-crossed couple on the screen finally made up and had their hot-and-heavy love scene.

Molly didn't seem to enjoy it. Her eyes glistened, in fact, almost as if she were close to tears. Definitely not the same response that the scene was getting from him.

Women were complicated.

Men were simple. They saw a woman they liked, they wanted sex. They watched sex, they wanted sex.

He glanced at her from the corner of his eye again.

She was beautiful and strong—no matter what she thought—and a great mother, honest, hardworking, sexy. He was mostly focused on the sexy part at the moment. Every cell of his body wanted her.

He couldn't take any more of the writhing bodies and throaty moaning on the TV. He got to his feet and retreated to the kitchen. He needed something cold. "Want a drink?"

"Sure. Thanks."

He stood in front of the open fridge door for a while,

letting the frigid air hit him, then grabbed the sweet-tea pitcher, poured two glasses and added ice. He also turned up the air-conditioning while he was walking by the thermostat.

She stood as she took the glass from him. "I think I'll go to bed early if you don't mind. I'm a little tired today."

Upset, she meant. He wished she would confide in him. She tried so damned hard to be strong. Too hard.

He set his glass on the sofa table and slowly pulled her into his arms. "What is it?"

"Just having a rough day." She put the glass down.

"I don't like seeing you sad."

"Mo…" She hesitated. "I should…"

"What?" He held her loosely, not wanting to scare her, not wanting to seem too pushy.

"Logan and I should probably move back home tomorrow."

Not what he wanted to hear. "Not yet. I like it when you're here," he admitted.

And that softened her face a little.

He reached up to brush the hair back from her eyes. Then rested his lips against her forehead, just savoring the feel of her in his arms. He wanted to keep her there forever, keep her safe from her troubles. "You know if there's anything I can help you with, I would, right? Whatever it is."

SHE WAS SO TEMPTED to tell him. But Kenny had said if she told anyone, her son would die. And that was a risk she wasn't willing to take.

If she told Mo, he would tell his team. His team would set up some kind of op. Her only experience with those was what she'd seen on TV shows. There'd be a shoot-out, probably.

There had been a shoot-out the night Dylan had died.

Her heart constricted.

She could deal with Kenny. Kenny wanted the drugs. She wanted Logan back. It would be a simple exchange. No fancy team of outsiders needed. The more people involved, the better chance that something could go wrong, someone could make a mistake.

She trusted Mo. She really did. To a point. She wanted to trust him all the way, but when her son was involved… she just couldn't make that final leap.

So she let him comfort her and kept quiet.

She leaned against him and soaked up his calm, self-assured energy. His steady heartbeat against her palm felt incredibly reassuring. He was a solid wall of strength.

"If you were in any kind of trouble, you would tell me, right?"

She nodded, unable to say the lie out loud.

He gathered her closer. Kissed her eyebrow.

She let him. Because when Mo found out that she had lied to him, that she helped Kenny, he would hate her.

The thought broke her heart. Because she'd been falling for him.

Starting tomorrow, she would be the enemy again, an accomplice in smuggling, for real this time. Back in the interrogation room without a doubt. But Logan would be safe from Kenny. Even if she got arrested, Grace would take care of her son. Logan would be safe. And that was worth whatever sacrifice Molly had to make.

So she said goodbye to Mo, silently, as he lowered his head and gently kissed her lips.

So unfair. They could have had something, she realized too late. He was different from all the other men she'd met. Images of what could have been flashed across her mind and took her breath away. Except, tomorrow he would hate her.

But she could have something, a little, tonight, a small voice said in her head. So she leaned into the kiss.

A low rumble sounded in his throat, a primal sound of passion that sent heat through her. He lifted her into his arms and headed straight to his bedroom with her. She didn't protest, just let him keep on kissing her.

He lay her on top of the covers as softly as if he thought she might break. Then he pulled his shirt over his head.

She sucked in a breath.

He was incredibly built. Action-movie stars had to paint on muscles to look like him. While he was fairly large, he didn't have an ounce of fat on his body, reminding her that she had curves sticking out every which way that she wished were much smaller.

She was a farm girl and she ate farm food, not designer protein shakes.

He stopped. "What's wrong?"

"I'm rethinking some of those pancake breakfasts."

"Don't," he said with a slow grin. "I'm pretty much crazy about your body."

That was news to her. "You are?"

He gave a strangled laugh as he lowered himself onto the giant bed next to her. "I can barely think every time I look at you. I wanted you while I was interrogating you." He covered his face with a hand as he lay on his back next to her. "How professional is that?"

Maybe not professional, but it was incredibly flattering.

"You never said anything."

He turned to his side and came up on one elbow. "You're a good woman. A mother. That needs to be respected."

A man who wanted her *and* respected her. And she was going to lose him tomorrow. She looked at the wall across from the bed and considered getting up to bang her head against it.

Instead, she reached up and pulled him down, fitting her mouth against his with a boldness she didn't know she possessed.

That was all the hint he needed.

He kissed her gently at first, tasting her lips. Then she opened for him and he accepted the invitation with enthusiasm. Hot need flooded her in an instant, pleasure surging through her.

The way he kissed her…almost reverently, but with so much heat and restrained passion. The sensations spreading through her made her head spin.

She was nearing thirty and she'd never truly been kissed. Not like this. The realization stunned her. And even scared her a little. Because she knew she was never again going to meet anyone like Mo.

She lifted her hands to his bare chest, her fingers gliding over the smooth skin that covered all those muscles.

His hand ran down her arm and up her belly, tugging her shirt upward. She wanted to feel his fingers on her bare skin. And then she did. His large hand covered half her abdomen, his heat burning through her skin. He caressed her gently, moving up inch by slow inch, stopping just under her breast.

Then his hand cupped her at last, and she arched into his touch. When he pulled his hand back, she almost protested before she realized he only pulled back to undo her shirt buttons so he could bare her to his gaze.

"I wish I knew just what to say," he said in a raspy whisper. "But you take my breath away."

Which was exactly the right thing to say.

Her shirt opened at last. She wished she owned something fancier than her simple white cotton bra. But he didn't seem to mind. He seemed mesmerized by it.

She lifted away from the bed a little so he could remove

the shirt, then held herself still while he fumbled with her bra clasp in the back.

"Not too good at this. Fingers too big," he said apologetically.

But she loved that he wasn't some skilled seducer, loved it that he wanted her so much it made his fingers tremble. He was Mo, exactly the man she wanted, needed.

Then she was naked to the waist and his eyes narrowed. Her nipples pebbled under his burning gaze. His head moved toward them as if drawn by a string.

The first touch of his lips against her hard nipple sent a hot flash of desire slicing through her. When he laved that nipple, heat pooled at the V of her thighs. Suddenly, she wanted things she didn't even know existed until now.

He was a steady man, one who liked to think things through, pay close attention to every step of the process. He brought those same skills to his lovemaking, leaving not a square inch of skin untouched, unkissed, driving her out of her mind with need.

She wished she'd met him before, not when everything was falling apart. She wished Dylan hadn't done what he'd done. She wished her life wasn't this complicated, that they could hold on to what they had here, that she didn't have to lie to him.

Then she pushed those thoughts away. If they were given only this night, she wasn't going to borrow trouble from tomorrow and poison what little time they had together.

Chapter Eleven

She was perfect. And for this moment, she was his.

What she made him feel…

He was old enough to know this kind of thing didn't come around all the time. Never before for him, in fact. And now that he had it, he didn't want to let her go. The only solution was to make her his forever. Starting right now, right here.

"A man could get used to this." Her soft skin felt like silk under his fingertips. She had enough curves to fill even his large hands, making him senseless with want. She fitted to him perfectly, as if she had been made for him.

She was passionate, responding to his every touch, arching her back, her eyes fluttering closed when he kissed her, then flying wide open when he touched her in her most intimate places. He reveled in that responsiveness, in the fact that he could make her feel that way.

He grinned at her. "You're good for me, you know that?"

For a second, her eyes cleared and something he couldn't identify flashed across them. Then she pulled his head down and kissed him silly again.

He had condoms in the nightstand drawer this time. He'd learned his lesson from the other day. He hadn't expected this to happen, but he'd been hoping.

He removed the rest of his clothing, and for a moment

they lay against each other, skin to skin. If that moment lasted a year, it wouldn't have been enough.

Then she parted her legs and drew her knee up over his hip, and the moment gained a sense of urgency.

He reached back, tore open a foil wrapper and sheathed himself then rolled her under him. "What have I done to deserve this?"

She tipped her head back and closed her eyes.

He moved to her opening, waited, for a moment finding it hard to believe this was happening, that she was giving herself to him like this. Then she lifted herself, welcoming him inside her body.

His eyes about rolled back in his head from the sharp pleasure. She was tight and wet for him. Moving.

Sweat broke out on his forehead.

"Molly." Her name came out in a strangled whisper.

And then he pushed, inch by slow inch, until he filled her to the hilt.

He could run twenty miles in full battle gear, but he was breathing hard now from that last little push. His heart beat against his ribs. He drew back, pushed in again, the friction increasing, his world spiraling out of control pretty damned rapidly.

He supported himself on his elbows as he dipped his head to kiss her, claiming those glorious lips again and again, their bodies rocking against each other, heat and pleasure building.

Then her body went taut and she gave a small cry, and the next thing he knew her muscles were contracting around him, pulsating, squeezing, sending him over the edge.

She blew his mind just absolutely, completely. When they lay side by side later, panting, all he could think was that he wanted to do this again as soon as possible.

He almost told her that, but somehow he wasn't sure if it would be romantic or just plain selfish, so he said nothing.

HER BONES MELTED. She'd never known sex could be like this. Wow. "Did that just happen?"

"And then some." He chuckled, sounding sated.

She'd always thought romantic movies and romance novels exaggerated. They had a product to sell, right?

But no. What they'd shared here, in Mo's bedroom, was all that and more, way beyond her wildest fantasies. He was a great guy. Her son liked him and looked up to him. And sex with him was out-of-this-world phenomenal.

And this was the end. She pressed closer.

Tomorrow he would hate her for lying to him.

The thought about killed her.

He drew her into his arms and kissed the top of her head.

His gentleness brought tears to her eyes. She hated lying to him. She had to press her lips together so the truth about Logan wouldn't burst out. So she stayed quiet and stayed close to him, soaking up the feeling while she could.

When he finally slept, she pulled away so she wouldn't disturb him with her tossing and turning and worrying about her son. She tried to remember the few times she'd been out to the mines. Could she find the right place?

Her grandfather had taken her out a few times, on horseback, to talk about the family's glory days. His grandfather and grand uncle had come to the area as poor miners. Between the two of them, they somehow scrimped together enough to buy partial stake in a small mine, eventually. They were successful for a while. Then they found out that the deposits weren't nearly as vast as advertised. They lost most of their money, bought land with what they had left and started ranching.

She thought about those old mine shafts, getting Logan back, losing Mo.

She passed out from sheer exhaustion toward dawn, but woke again a little while later. She slipped from the bed at first light, grabbed her clothes and dressed in the bathroom. She shut down all emotion, left a note for Mo on the kitchen counter, then sneaked away.

Couldn't sleep. Went out to the ranch. I'll ask Grace to come over with me.

Mo READ THE NOTE over for the second time.

Grace Cordero, an army vet, was definitely good enough for bodyguard duty. But he would have liked to spend the morning with Molly.

Did she have second thoughts about what had happened last night? He hoped not. He'd liked every minute and wanted more. And not just the sex. He wanted more of her. All of her.

But it seemed she wanted space.

Okay. Fine. Whatever she needed. He was in this for the long haul. So he drank his coffee, got dressed and went into the office.

SHE DIDN'T CALL GRACE. She didn't want anyone else involved in her lies. She didn't need a bodyguard. She knew now who sent the men who'd searched her ranch: Kenny. And he was waiting for word from her on the whereabouts of the drugs. She took care of her animals in record time. They seemed agitated.

The horizon was a threatening shade of purplish-gray when she came out of the barn with her milk pails. Looked as if a storm was coming, she thought as she finished up.

A bad storm could wipe out half her gardens. She

couldn't worry about that now. She only cared about Logan today and his well-being. "I'm coming, baby," she muttered under her breath, trying not to let desperation get the better of her.

She hurried to her pickup and rode out on the dirt road that wound its way through the fields.

She knew the mine openings were to the east of the house. She sort of knew where they were in relation to each other. Once she found one, she was pretty sure she could find the rest.

Heat shimmered over the land, the vegetation dry, dust blowing from the bare patches. A dust devil rose up on the road right in front of her. She drove around it and scanned the land, followed her memories and, after some false starts, found the first opening.

She pulled up next to the pile of rocks that had some old two-by-fours and rebar sticking out. Rubble covered the ground, some scraggly weeds growing in the dirt the winds had deposited between the rocks over the years. Didn't look as if anybody had been here since the shaft had been blown in.

At least she was in the general area. "Hang in there, Logan," she whispered into the wind. "I'm coming."

She drove around in expanding circles, looking for another entry. She found one half an hour later, looking the same as the first. Then another one that obviously hadn't been disturbed in ages, either. Doubt began to fill her, cold panic spreading through her limbs.

The mines *had* to be the answer. This had to be it, because she had no other ideas, and her son's life depended on her locating the stupid drugs Kenny wanted.

She had trouble finding the next shaft, maybe because she was becoming more and more frazzled. She was praying out loud as she drove and almost missed the spot. The opening was covered with dry brush. She only recognized the place because of the car-size rocks by a nearby mesquite grove. She recalled trips with her grandfather, sitting on those rocks in the shade and drinking water out of his canteen, eating homemade beef jerky.

The dry brush, carried here from someplace else, gave her hope. It certainly looked as if someone had tried to camouflage the spot.

She jumped out of her pickup and began dragging those dead bushes away. Under the brush, a faded brown tarp covered a rusty set of metal doors, the kind people used for outside basement entries. She zeroed in on the padlock. New.

Every instinct she had screamed that this was it.

A small voice inside said it wasn't too late to call Mo. She almost did. But no, she shoved her cell phone back into her pocket.

She was so close. She could do it. Her son's safety was the most important thing here, and if Kenny thought she brought anyone in, who knew what he would do. She would have never thought he could hurt a kid, but then again, she would have never thought he could be involved in smuggling, either.

She kicked the padlock in frustration. A lock cutter would have been nice. She didn't have that, but she did have a tire iron in the back of the pickup. So she ran to get that and used it to bust the lock, grunting and sweating in the heat, but refusing to give up until the metal gave.

Then she threw open the rusty doors and looked into the darkness. A makeshift wooden ramp led down, a flashlight conveniently sitting on the top step. She left it there. She had no idea how good the battery was. She had a newly charged flashlight in her glove compartment and she went to get that.

She turned on the flashlight then followed the ramp.

Fist-size spiders hung on the walls and above her head. She could hear something scurrying up ahead, then nearly stepped on a rattlesnake.

"Easy. I'm not here to hurt you." She backed around it carefully, grateful that it had sounded its rattle to warn her.

She wiped her forehead with her free hand, moving forward even more carefully, especially when she remembered how fond Dylan had been of booby traps. She felt as if she was in an Indiana Jones movie, half expected poisoned darts to shoot out of the walls, or the ceiling to start pressing down on her. She really hated dark, ominous places.

She moved forward anyway. She found no traps, just discarded beer cans here and there. Budweiser. Her brother's favorite. Disappointment choked her.

"Dammit, Dylan." She kicked a can that bounced far ahead, the sound echoing off the walls. She followed after it.

She only had to go in a few hundred feet before she saw the two crates, the wood slats new, unlike the blackened supports of the old mine shaft. These crates had been a recent addition to the place, and she knew what they held without having to pry one open. She'd let Kenny do that.

She walked back out of the mine shaft so she could get reception for her phone, then called him, giving him directions on how to find her.

"I knew you could do this, darling. You just stay where you are, now. I'm bringing the boy," he promised.

Mo spent his morning on the border, but when he had to head into Hullett to check on something and had to drive close by the Rogers ranch on his way into town, he decided to stop in. He was willing to give Molly the space she needed to think, but he wanted to make sure she was okay.

Her pickup wasn't in the driveway, but he got out and checked around the buildings anyway. The chickens were out, all the animals fed and watered. She'd gotten an early start and had probably finished early. Made sense. She was most likely back in Hullett by now.

He drove into town and decided to swing by his place, but only the dogs greeted him.

"Hey, are you here?" He walked through the empty living room and kitchen, back to her room. Knocked on her door. "Are you in there?"

No answer.

He knocked again then pushed the door in. Her room stood empty. Maybe she'd gone to pick up Logan from his sleepover. He grabbed a cookie and a cold drink then headed over to the sheriff's office.

Ryder called just as Mo pulled out of the underground parking garage. "Hey, I caught up with the informant we have on the other side of the border."

"Yeah?" he asked absentmindedly, weaving through traffic, thinking about Molly.

"He says the Pebble Creek sheriff is over there a lot. He likes cockfights."

That had Mo sitting up and paying attention. "If he has a gambling problem—if some criminal has him in his debt—"

"They might be able to call in some favors," Ryder finished for him. "At the very least, get him to turn a blind eye."

Mo rubbed the back of his neck. "I don't like the guy. I can see him being up to no good. He's shifty."

"Maybe. Don't go convicting the sheriff yet just because the man is sweet on Molly Rogers."

Mo coughed. "I don't know what you're talking about. I'm not the jealous type."

"Sure. That's why your head turned blue the other day when Keith told you the sheriff's car was in her driveway."

He didn't want to go there. But talking about Molly... He hesitated for a second before he asked, "Have you seen Grace today yet?"

"Sure."

"She didn't mention anything about Molly being upset this morning, did she?"

"Why would Molly Rogers be upset?"

He didn't want to go there, either. "Just thought, you know, since Grace helped her at the ranch this morning, she might have mentioned something to you."

"Grace didn't go to the Rogers ranch this morning."

"Early. Maybe before you stopped by her place. Around six."

A moment of silence passed. "Grace was with me at six. And before six, too."

Meaning that he'd spent the night with Grace. Unease skittered down Mo's spine.

"Is something wrong?" Ryder asked.

"I don't think so. Just got our wires crossed, probably."

But as soon as he hung up with Ryder, he dialed Molly. He should have called her sooner, but didn't want to crowed her if she needed a little time to process what had happened between them last night. He didn't want her to think he was pushing her into anything.

The call rang out, but she didn't pick up. Which didn't necessarily mean trouble. Could be she was just ignoring him. He was almost hoping that was the case.

He sure didn't like the alternative.

SHE DIDN'T TAKE Mo's call. She didn't want to lie to him again. It was almost over.

She kept her eyes on the approaching black van in the

distance and the dust cloud that followed it. She slid off the rock she used to sit on as a kid and left the shade of the mesquite grove, hurried over to the pickup, reached in through the open window and beeped her horn to guide Kenny in the right direction.

Endless, agonizing seconds passed before he reached close enough so she could see Logan in the passenger seat. Then she could fully fill her lungs for the first time since he hadn't stepped off the school bus yesterday.

Logan was here. He looked okay. Everything would be fine now.

She ran to the van as soon as Kenny stopped, got her son out and grabbed him up into her arms, kissing him silly. "Are you okay?"

He held on to her neck for all he was worth, didn't protest about being a big boy or any of that.

She never wanted to let him out of her arms again. "Did anyone hurt you?"

He shook his head, keeping a brave face, but there were smudged tear tracks on his little cheeks. "Can we go home, Mom?"

"Yes, we can." She set him down, took his hand and walked toward her pickup with him when Kenny said, "I'd like to see what you have here first."

"It's down there." She pointed at the open metal doors.

"I'd rather that you came with me." Then he added, "The kid, too."

He might not have brought his police cruiser, but he did bring his service revolver. He glanced at the gun in the holster at his side, then at her, without saying anything.

Her pickup waited a few steps away. If they ran... But they'd be sitting ducks while they got in and she started the engine. She didn't want to give Kenny a reason to do something stupid. She would do whatever it took to stop the situation from escalating into violence.

So she held her son's hand and walked to the dark hole. "It's fine. Almost done." She did her best to reassure him, holding on to him as they went down together.

Kenny followed right behind them, picking up the extra flashlight.

She skirted around the snake, keeping herself between it and Logan, trying not to make a big deal of the move, hoping Kenny would step right on the rattler. But he was paying attention, pulled his gun and blew the snake's head clear off.

The sound was deafening in the tunnel. Logan held on to her tightly. "Mom?"

"It's okay. Just a snake, honey." She led Kenny to the two crates, panned them with the flashlight, ready to turn and leave.

But Kenny said, "Where is the rest?"

Her stomach sank. This couldn't be happening. "What rest?"

"I'm looking for a lot more than this. I need the full shipment."

The shaft stretched in front of them, breaking off into several corridors up ahead. Would Dylan leave these two crates here as a decoy? Maybe for the authorities, in case they found his hiding place? Then he would hide the bulk of his hoard in a place more difficult to reach. Possibly.

"Maybe the rest are farther in," she suggested, just as Kenny's light went out.

He banged it against the heel of his hand, but nothing happened. He tossed it aside and grabbed hers then strode forward. "Let's find the damned things."

"You don't need us for this. Please let us go. It's all yours now, Kenny."

But he gestured for her to walk ahead of him. "Just to make sure you delivered what you promised."

For a second the beam of the flashlight hit his face and she saw his expression, regret mixed with determination.

"Go ahead. And make sure the kid sticks close to you."

The kid. He hadn't called Logan by name once. He hadn't called her by name, either, not on the phone, not since he'd gotten here.

Because he is distancing himself. A chill ran down her spine.

"Just let us go. All I want is Logan. I won't ever say a word about this to anyone. I swear."

His gaze fell on her son. "We'll find the crates together."

Fear sliced through her when she understood at last. Kenny didn't plan on letting Logan and her leave.

"Go," he snapped, getting impatient.

Panic filled her as she stumbled forward, her fingertips going numb. Why hadn't she thought of this before? Of course he wouldn't let them go. She was a witness. She knew that the Pebble Creek sheriff was involved in smuggling. He couldn't risk that she would tell someone about it. And even if he thought she could keep her mouth shut, there was Logan. He wouldn't trust a kid to keep his secret.

God, she'd been an idiot.

She'd been so focused on getting Logan back. And Kenny had been her brother's friend. She'd known the man all her life. She simply hadn't thought he would cross that line. Harming anyone, let alone a kid, was so unimaginable to her, she had trouble believing someone she knew would do something like that.

A naive and dangerous way to be.

Dylan had been ready to shoot Grace. She no longer doubted that Grace was telling the truth about that. Bitterness rose in her throat. This was what money and greed

did to people—turned them into something you no longer
recognized.

"Kenny, you can't—"

"Keep going."

She should have trusted Mo. She squeezed her eyes shut
for a second. She should have told him what was going on.
Mo would have helped her.

She shoved her free hand into her pocket. If she could
get off a text message to Mo without Kenny noticing… She
glanced at the display. She had zero reception down here.

No calls going out, no calls coming in.

It was too late.

Mo LOOKED AT the finger-challenged gangbanger in the interrogation room then shoved the table aside. The man had
been questioned by both Shep and CBP but had refused to
talk. Gang code or whatever.

Jose Caballo. He was the one who'd stabbed Garcia Cruz
to death, as it turned out. He'd been using his victim's ID
as a joke.

"I'm only going to ask one more time. Why did you
slash Molly Rogers's tires? What were you doing there?"

The man flashed him a dispassionate look.

Mo slammed the bastard against the wall, shoving his
thumb into just the right spot between the man's vertebrae.

Jose gave a shout of pain.

"How is the bottom half of your body feeling?" Mo
whispered into the man's ear. "Feel anything?" He waited
as the man moaned. "I didn't think so." He pushed harder.
"I can make it so you'll never have feeling down there
again."

Sweat rolled down the man's face.

"Kiss the chicas goodbye, amigo," Mo went on. "Then
again, women aren't going to be a big problem for you any-

way, not when you're going to federal prison for murder. Plenty of gangs there. And you in a wheelchair. Hell, I sure wouldn't want to be defenseless like that."

Jose's lips were turning white.

"What were you looking for at the Rogers ranch?" Mo asked.

And for the first time, the man spoke. "Drugs."

"Who sent you? Who told you to scare her?"

"Nobody. I got my fingers chopped for that. I was just supposed to find the drugs. She wasn't supposed to know. I got angry when I didn't find anything."

She wasn't supposed to know. Just like the other men in the barn, using a Taser instead of a gun. As if whoever sent them made sure to tell them Molly shouldn't get hurt.

In the back of his mind, puzzle pieces shuffled and revealed a picture he didn't like. He needed to know for sure if he was right. "Who do you work for? Is it Sheriff Davis?"

The man squeezed his eyes shut and pressed his lips together. The pain had to be close to unbearable.

Molly was missing.

Mo pushed harder.

"Yes." The man bit out the words then dropped at Mo's feet.

He left him, strode past a couple of cops in the hallway. "He passed out. Probably low blood pressure. Might want to give him a cup of water."

Then he drove to the office for extra guns and ammo and a quick powwow with his team.

"Something kept pricking my instincts about him, but I thought it was just because the man was putting moves on Molly." He'd called already, but Kenny was off duty and couldn't be reached. Same as Molly. He swore, frustration and worry filling him.

"She could be at the hairdresser or whatever, with her phone turned off," Jamie suggested.

Mo shook his head. Molly was in trouble. He could feel it in his bones, and it drove him crazy.

Ryder's face darkened. "Hey, we've all been working in this field long enough to respect instinct. If you say something's wrong, something's wrong. What do you want to do?"

"Track her cell phone." It was the best idea he could come up with during the ride back from Hullett. "I'd like to know where she is. If her car is parked in front of some hair salon…" But he knew it wouldn't be.

"What's her number?" Shep asked, bringing up the satellite log-in.

Mo rattled it off.

Shep entered it. "It's going to take a couple of minutes."

"We can track Kenny Davis's car, too. All the police cruisers have trackers," Jamie said. "That might go faster."

Shep worked his keyboard for a few interminably long minutes. "Okay, got the tracking code for the car." He typed something into the keyboard. Waited, then looked up, his face grim. "The sheriff's cruiser is parked in front of the police station. He's using another vehicle."

"Want me to call in Keith and Ray?" Ryder offered.

Mo shook his head. "Let's see first if we have anything." But he knew they did. He checked the pistol he normally carried, then grabbed his two backup weapons from his desk drawer and holstered up.

"Last known location is her ranch, right?" Jamie asked. "Any sign of struggle there?"

"No."

"All right. Satellite response. Here's Molly." Shep turned his screen around, and Mo leaned closer. The image showed the borderlands with a red dot in the middle of nowhere.

"That's on the Rogers ranch." Mo recognized the section of the map immediately. He'd studied it enough in the past few weeks. "Can you tell how long she's been there?"

"Actually, that's not a current reading. It's from about an hour ago."

"What about now?"

"Nothing. The signal disappeared."

"Pretty close to the border," Shep observed. "If she is involved in something…"

The Rio Grande, a dark line snaking through the landscape, rolled just a little to the south.

"No." Mo entered the coordinates into his phone's GPS then strode for the door. "She's in trouble. I don't know what's going on, but there's something wrong about this."

Ryder kicked his chair back, reaching for his weapon on his desk. "Don't think you're going to have all the fun."

They all followed after him, each going to his own SUV. His team, Mo thought. It was the darndest thing. They'd only been a team for a few months. He barely knew them. Other than a security detail once or twice here in the U.S. under special circumstances, he'd done lone-wolf operations, mostly overseas, for most of his career.

He didn't figure himself for a team guy. He'd never even played team sports. In high school, he'd done weight lifting. The funny feeling that caught him now, as the others all lined up to follow him on a hunch, caught him unexpectedly.

"I appreciate this," he called out as they all jumped into their SUVs.

They didn't dillydally on the road, either. They were on the Rogers ranch in record time, then off-roading it to the GPS coordinates. A storm gathered, dark clouds rolling across the sky.

Dammit, Molly. He'd sensed that something wasn't quite

right last night, but had let lust carry him away instead of pushing her for answers. And that note this morning… He should have called her sooner. He wished she could have trusted him enough to ask for his help.

He'd thought they were closer.

But obviously she didn't share the feeling. Which bothered him for a number of reasons.

He spotted her pickup and headed straight for it, worried about the van parked just a few feet away. No windows in the back, license plate smeared with dirt, nondescript dark color. The type of car used by people who didn't want to be noticed. Because they were up to no good. *Hell*.

He pulled up hard, jumped out, then the others were there, too, half a minute later. That he didn't know what was going on just about killed him.

"What's this?" Jamie hurried forward, toward the hole in the ground, catching up with Mo.

Mo's muscles tightened. "Old mine shaft." The county was riddled with them. Most of them were completely unsafe, nothing but death traps. Which was why they were kept blocked off, usually.

"You knew about this?" Ryder wanted to know.

He shook his head. "Whatever is going on here, Molly is not a willing participant."

Jamie looked at the sky. "It's going to rain soon," he observed casually. "Getting trapped underground in torrential rains wouldn't be the smartest thing."

Ryder called in Keith and Ray for backup, but nobody was about to wait for them.

"Better get her up and out of here fast." Mo drew his gun and went down the ramp first, pulled the standard military-issue flashlight off his belt. He saw a dead snake that had recently met with a bullet. He kicked it aside. A little farther in, two wooden crates stood in the middle of the path. Beyond that, the shaft went on for a few hundred feet before branching off in several directions.

"Looks like we found our drugs," Ryder said.

Mo passed by the crates without looking at them twice. "Now let's find Molly. And keep an eye out for her son, too," he added on instinct. He could only think of one reason why Molly would be down here, with crates of drugs.

He'd bet his Cat Counting company shares Logan was in trouble.

They hurried forward, stopped at the intersection of tunnels, four shafts for the four of them. They didn't waste time arguing over whether to stick together or split up. They were tough commando soldiers; each could handle pretty much anything on their own.

Mo took the shaft that went straight forward, gun in one hand, flashlight in the other.

Thunder sounded above and the earth shook as lightning struck. Dirt snowed on his head, underscoring the fact that the old structure wasn't exactly stable. He just hoped it held long enough to rescue Molly and Logan.

Chapter Twelve

They had precious little light to see by. The surrounding
darkness was oppressive, a heavy presence pushing down
on them. The air smelled musty. The deeper they went,
the more the temperature dropped. *Cold as a grave.* Molly
shook off the thought. She had to keep it together. She had
to figure out a way to escape or they'd be killed.

"Faster," Kenny ordered. "I have other things to do
today."

"I can barely see where I'm going." She had no inten-
tion of hurrying. She needed time to think.

As soon as they found the rest of the crates, he would
shoot them, like he had shot the snake, she thought as they
passed yet another shaft, this one going straight down.
When Kenny shined the light into the hole, she could see
water about seven or eight feet below.

This part of her ranch lay higher than the lands a little
farther south, where the Rio Grande rushed to the east,
but was still low enough for her to wonder if the rain that
threatened would come and when. She had plans to escape
from Kenny, and she didn't plan on drowning.

"Not down there, I'm guessing," Kenny said as he passed
by the hole. "Keep moving."

Then they reached another central spot that led to multiple shafts. A giant mass loomed up ahead in one of them,

a dark shadow that reached from the floor to the ceiling. They found the rest of the crates.

"Good," Kenny said with a dose of relief. "We lost too much money in the factory raid. Your brother ponied up for that. If this got lost, I'd have to pay for it."

Pain bubbled up in her heart. Dylan… She shook her head. Was that why he'd mortgaged the ranch? Didn't matter now. She couldn't worry about that at the moment. She had to figure out a way to survive this.

As Kenny panned the crates with the flashlight, she caught the glint of a thin wire a few feet in front of them. Only because she'd been looking, because she'd been expecting it. Kenny didn't seem to notice the booby trap. So Dylan *had* protected his treasure.

She had a split second to make a decision. She gave Logan's hand a squeeze, a silent warning. Then she spun around and kicked the flashlight from Kenny's hand, doing her best to copy the move she'd seen Mo teach Logan.

Miraculously, she hit her target. The next second they were plunged into darkness.

"Quick!" She dragged her son down a shaft, away from the crates, running forward in the pitch dark and praying they didn't fall. Her only goal was to get as far from Kenny and that wire as possible.

"Get back here!" Kenny shouted, swearing after them.

Then he found the flashlight and shone the light around. She saw another shaft to her left. She dragged Logan into it, into the darkness and out of Kenny's line of sight.

With a little luck, he would want to check the crates first.

She ran forward, stumbling, catching herself. "Hurry!"

Logan didn't have to be told twice. He ran as fast as his little legs could carry him. Soccer practice paid off, obviously. He ran just as fast as she did.

She only wished she could see better. She was completely disoriented in the dark, hoping the tunnel was straight so she wouldn't run face first into a wall. She kept a step in front of Logan, so at least she could save him from injury. If she crashed, she would just have to pick herself up and keep going.

They were both breathing hard, wheezing for air that was musty and humid this deep inside the shaft.

The explosion, when it came, knocked her off her feet.

THE GROUND-SHAKING boom didn't come from lightning above. This was an explosion, underground, and it scared the spit out of Mo. He'd seen plenty of explosions in his life, had been the cause of a number of them.

But this time, Molly's life was at stake, and possibly Logan's.

At least the sound told him in what direction to run. He picked up speed, ready for anything, panning the light over the ground then on the ceiling to make sure he wasn't running headfirst into a tunnel that was collapsing.

Then, after an eternity, he spotted another light up ahead and soon made out the form of a man sitting, heard him cough from the dust that filled the air. Behind him, the tunnel was filled with rubble.

Mo pushed forward. "Sheriff?"

Only then did the man notice him, looking up with a startled expression on his face. But before Mo could ask where Molly was, the Pebble Creek sheriff swung his arm around and opened fire.

Bam. Bam. Bam. The acrid smell of gun smoke filled the dusty air.

Mo tossed his flashlight that did nothing at this stage but make him a target, then returned fire. Kenny was smart enough to turn off his own light the next instant. The two of them shot at each other blindly, bullets ricocheting off the rock walls.

God, this was stupid.

"Molly?" Mo called out in the dark. Just because he hadn't seen her didn't mean she hadn't been back there somewhere in the shadows. He didn't want to hit her accidently.

But no response came.

Shots peppered the air for about another minute. Then nothing. Looked as if they ran out of bullets at the same time.

He shoved his empty gun into the back of his waistband and lurched forward, groping for Kenny. Beams creaked above them, an ominous sound. But even over that, he could hear the bastard's wheezing.

That led him to the man, and Mo grabbed him by the shoulders, from the feel of it. "Where is she?"

"Go to hell." Kenny kicked out, bringing them to the stone-covered ground.

Rolling on that didn't feel too good, as sharp shards shredded Mo's skin. He tried to keep on top of Kenny as much as possible. The sheriff was in pretty good shape and trained in hand-to-hand combat, putting up a damned good fight. He was lighter than Mo and quicker. But in the end Mo's sheer muscle-mass advantage got the better of him.

"Where is she?" He slammed the man into the ground and felt something wet on the back of his hands. Probably blood. Couldn't tell which one of them was bleeding.

Kenny coughed. "Ran into a tunnel."

"Which one?"

Kenny only laughed at that.

"Where is she?" Mo demanded again and shook him harder, but the man's body went slack.

This time Kenny didn't cough, just wheezed. He didn't

fight back, either. Maybe he'd caught a bullet. "Don't know. Got away."

He'd find her. "Who sends the drugs over?" Mo asked next.

This was the closest his team had gotten to something real. Dylan Rogers had died before he could have been questioned. "Who is Coyote?"

Kenny wheezed.

"Tell me how I find the guy, and I'll get you out of here," Mo promised. "Or I'm leaving and you can bleed out in this hellhole, wondering if the rats or the collapsing ceiling will get to you first."

The beams groaned, underscoring his words.

Kenny gave a weak cough, his body completely limp now. "Coyote," he said, his hand coming up to grab Mo's wrist.

"Who is he?"

But Kenny's hand fell away, each breath shallower than the one before it.

"Don't you die, you damned traitor." Mo swore.

"Needed the money." Kenny gasped. "Doesn't hurt anybody. If I don't do it, someone else will."

"Bringing terrorists into the country doesn't hurt anybody?"

"Just drugs and guns. Some illegals."

Mo shook him again, running out of patience. "What do you know about the terrorists?"

"Nobody's coming in." He took a break to wheeze. "It's all on hold."

They already knew that. But now something new occurred to Mo. Once Coyote let his dogs loose, they'd rush to make up for the lost income. A sudden influx of contraband would keep CBP busy. Busy enough so that someplace unexpected, a small group of terrorists could be sneaked across the border. Sure looked as if all this was part of a grand plan.

He gripped the man's shoulders. "Until when is everything on hold? When can you start up again?"

But the sheriff seemed past talking.

Mo let the man go and searched for his flashlight, found it after a few minutes of mad groping. "Talk to me, dammit." He aimed the light at Kenny.

A gunshot wound bloomed in the middle of the man's chest.

"When?" he demanded.

For a second, Kenny's eyes slid open. "Help," he gasped. "I'm dying."

"At least don't die a traitor." But he wasn't sure the bastard heard him. His eyes closed again.

Mo shook him. Nothing. The sheriff was completely out of it, dammit. There'd be no answers coming from him.

Mo gritted his teeth while the mine rumbled around them as cracks ran through the tunnels, the shock waves from the explosion destabilizing the entire structure.

He needed to get to Molly. A half-dozen shafts opened from the main tunnel he'd followed here. No time to make mistakes. Which one to take?

A scraping sound came from behind him.

He swung the flashlight that way. "Molly?"

Skipper bounded out of the darkness, giving an anxious bark.

"How did you get here?"

He knew the answer before Skipper jumped up on him, barking, licking his face. Ryder had called Grace, and she had come with the dog. Thank God.

He ruffled Skipper's fur. "Find Molly. Come on, girl. Where's Logan?"

The dog's intelligent eyes glistened in the semidarkness. She sniffed around then darted down the closest shaft.

Mo ran after her. "Molly!"

And somewhere, far ahead, he heard a scream.

The sound cut right through his heart. He ran. Then he ran harder. He was running for the woman he was falling in love with, dammit.

The few minutes until he found her seemed an eternity. They huddled in the dark a hundred feet ahead of him, looking like statues, covered in gray dust. Skipper was whining and prodding them with her nose. And then the tangle of limbs moved. His heart dared beat again.

"Are you two okay?" He held his breath for the answer.

"Some of the dirt came down. I thought it would bury us." She shook dust from her head, then ruffled Logan's hair to clean him off.

He helped them stand. They could move. Okay. Good. Nothing looked broken. He pulled them up into his arms, held them tight, Skipper muscling her way into the middle. "Did Kenny have anyone with him?"

"He was alone." Molly's voice was more than a little shaky. "What are you doing here with Skipper? How did you find us?"

"Long story. I'll tell you later."

The mine groaned and creaked all around them, an ominous boom sounding in the distance.

"Run!" He grabbed for her hand. She tugged Logan after her, and they moved as fast as was possible under the circumstances, the dog running ahead, barking.

When they reached Kenny, Mo panned the light over the man. He *had* promised to take him out. But Kenny was no longer breathing. His eyes gazed off into nothing.

Then Mo caught something in the dust next to him. Some scribbles: *10 1*. His mind registered the numbers before Skipper walked all over the writing and erased it. She sniffed Kenny, nudged him with her nose a couple of times, then walked back to Logan.

October first.

But what did the date mean? They needed the information Kenny could have given them. Too late. And no time to worry over it. Mo kept moving.

He had to focus on what could still be saved. "We have to hurry."

Except, somehow the force of the explosion traveled through certain layers of rock and collapsed the tunnel ahead of them, too, he realized as he panned ahead with his flashlight. They were in some kind of a pocket, held up as if by a miracle.

They stared at the pile of rocks that blocked their way, only a small hole open on top. And that not for long, Mo saw. The entire structure was unstable. The rest would come down if any of them tried to climb up there.

Molly stepped forward. "We can push through." Panic tinged her voice.

"No." He held her back. Then gave her the truth straight-out, because she deserved to know. "This whole level is collapsing."

COLD FEAR PARALYZED HER. "We have to get out," she begged, her gaze fixed on that little hole. They could squeeze through there. She knew they could. It was the way they had come in. They needed to get out. *Now.*

But Mo pulled her back again. "Not that way."

"There's no other way!"

"There was a shaft going down, to a lower level."

That hole with the water at the bottom? That made no sense. She didn't want to go down, deeper into the earth. She wanted to go up. Her panic and every instinct she had pushed her toward that small gap in the rubble. If they could crawl through there…

Skipper could help with the digging. She was a great digger. "Come on, Skipper."

But Skipper was backing away.

"Listen to me," Mo said in that steady voice of his. "Trust me."

Trust? Oh, God, now? She was nearly blind with fear, ready to bolt like a scared animal.

Yet on some level… She closed her eyes for a second. Drew a deep breath. *This is Mo,* she thought. *This is Mo.* He wanted to protect her. She didn't doubt that. Did she trust him to know what he was doing?

She wanted to trust him. She swallowed hard. "Okay."

And then she let him lead her and her son back, to the hole that freaked her out completely.

The ceiling shook above them. Water glistened below. Just above the level of the water, an opening gaped in the side of the vertical drop, the entry to another horizontal tunnel, parallel to theirs. The remains of a wooden ladder clung to the wall of the down shaft, pretty thoroughly rotted. No way could they step on that.

"So we just drop? Then what?"

"We don't drop. There could be something in that water, a sharp beam. Don't want anyone to get skewered." He lay on the ground and leaned in, panned the hole with his flashlight. "I'll lower you down. Come on. You first. Logan? Can you hold the flashlight, buddy?"

Logan stared at her, too shaken to move.

"It's like the next level in a video game," Mo told him, his voice steady and gentle. "That's the level that takes us out of here. Then we win."

Logan nodded at last and took the flashlight from him, angled it at the hole below them.

Mo took her hands, lowered her, swung her toward the opening. She lunged for her target, landed on her knees, probably lost some skin, but it was the least of her worries. An inch or two of water covered the bottom. Other than that, she couldn't see much of the shaft.

"Ready?" His voice came from above.

She moved back to the opening, caught the flashlight Mo tossed her and set it down so it illuminated the entry and he would know what to aim for. "Yes." And then she caught Logan as Mo swung him.

He came next, lowering himself handhold by handhold while beams fell above.

"Come on, Skipper. Jump!" He held out his arms as soon as his feet were on solid ground.

Skipper whined above.

"Jump!" Logan shouted.

And the dog lunged into the hole while Molly held her breath.

Mo caught her, dragged her into the shaft with them.

And then the mine shuddered around them once again. It felt like an earthquake. Rocks fell down the drop they'd just come down. Dust filled the space as the upper level collapsed, everything shaking.

They held their breaths, Mo sheltering them from the falling debris with his great body. But that was all, just some earth and small rocks. Their level held.

"Let's get out of here," he said as soon as the tremors stopped.

Skipper led them, and they followed her, coughing up dust, sloshing through rising water. Must be raining up on top, on the surface. It didn't look good. In fact, it didn't look as if they were going to make it.

She squeezed her son's hand. "Good job. I love you."

Logan looked up to her. "I love you, too, Mom."

She bit her lip as she turned to Mo. "I'm sorry I didn't tell you about Kenny. I'm sorry about everything."

It needed to be said. She had never been as happy as when she heard Mo's voice calling for her back there. "I know you're mad at me, but I can explain—"

"I'm not mad at you." He took her hand and held it. "Are you okay there, buddy? You're not scared, are you?" he asked Logan.

"It's like a video game, right?" Logan asked with a measure of uncertainty, but he held it together.

Skipper stuck to him like glue. That probably helped a lot.

"It's exactly like that," Mo reassured her son with full confidence. "And guess what? We're definitely winning."

"We are?"

"Do I know about video games or what?"

And then Logan gave a little smile, and Molly's heart melted. Whether they were really winning or not, he took her son's fear away and that was a big thing.

They slogged forward for what seemed an eternity, found other tunnels. Mo moved forward without hesitation each time. Now and then, he let Skipper guide them.

"How do you know which way to go?" Logan asked.

"I have a pretty good sense of direction. And so does your dog. If there's fresh air coming in anywhere up ahead, she can smell it."

Molly gave thanks for that. Maybe they did have a slim chance. If they could outrun the water.

"How many entrances to the mine?" Mo asked her.

"Half dozen, but other than the one we came through, the rest are sealed."

"They can be unsealed. We have backup. If we can't find a way up, they'll come for us. Very likely most of the shafts are connected."

Okay. That made her feel better.

He stopped when they reached air that wasn't so filled with dust. It seemed the explosion hadn't shaken this section. He pulled out his phone.

"No reception down here," she told him.

"That's fine. I'm activating an emergency beacon."

"Will that work?"

"You bet. It's new technology we just started testing. A new generation of the technology they use in black boxes in airplanes."

That sounded encouraging. Authorities could find black boxes all the way on the bottom of the ocean after planes crashed. They should be able to find them here. A little more hope came to life inside her.

"I'd appreciate it if you didn't mention this to anyone," Mo said to the both of them. "It's still experimental and kind of a government secret."

"Sure," she promised.

While Logan said, "It's like a spy video game," looking wide-eyed and impressed.

Truth be told, she was no less excited about the gadget. But as they moved on, it occurred to her how strange it was that he would have something like that. Why would a policy-recommendation team test top technology such as this? *Secret* technology.

Not for the first time, she had the sneaky suspicion his team was more than what they seemed. Not a topic to bring up in front of Logan, obviously.

They'd been sloshing through water that was an inch or two deep, but suddenly it was reaching to midcalf, rising rapidly now. Either the tunnel slanted down or rain was coming down pretty hard above. She tightened her hold on Mo's hand.

He looked back at her, then at the water and squeezed

back as if saying *It's fine.* He had noticed her apprehension. She should have known. He missed little.

He kept on moving forward, and she followed, instead of backing up to higher ground. She had decided she would trust him, and so she would. She would trust him with her life and with her son's, because he'd earned her trust and because she was in love with him.

The admission shook her as hard as the explosion had.

But she was jarred out of her daze when his cell phone pinged.

"What's that?" Logan asked as Skipper let out a woof.

"A sign that the rescue team is coming for us." Mo looked at the screen. "From that direction." He pointed straight ahead. "Might as well meet them halfway, if you can keep going."

"Yep," Logan said.

"We're fine," Molly added. The sooner they were above ground, the better.

But the going was slow over the uneven ground. Here and there they had to crawl over old rubble. Nearly an hour passed before they met the rescue detail, Ryder and Shep. By then, the water was up to their knees.

Ryder scooped up Logan.

Mo scooped up Molly.

And then the going got quite a bit faster. The men moved like a well-oiled machine.

They reached a shaft that led up, a rope hanging down, Jamie looking down on them from above. Ryder climbed easily with Logan on his back. Shep tossed a squirming Skipper across his shoulders and Skipper lay flat, if whining a little.

Mo put Molly down and turned his back to her. "Piggyback ride. Get on."

She hesitated.

"We don't have time for this," he reminded her gently. The water reached midthigh.

She set aside her pride and climbed on, her arms around his neck, but not too tight. He took them up without effort and didn't put her down when they reached the top, just started running with her.

As the light of his flashlight wobbled in front of them, she could see why. Several support beams had fallen. The tunnel could collapse at any second.

And then it did, just as Mo dived through the opening with her, out into the night lit up by car beams all around them.

Rain lashed at her face as they lay side by side, gasping for air. Hands reached for them, Logan plowing into her before she had a chance to stand, knocking the both of them into the mud. Mo pulled them up.

Grace was there somewhere, asking how they were, what she could do to help. Skipper was licking Logan's face.

"I got them," Mo said, his voice rough.

Grace got in a hug anyway. "Friends don't give friends gray hair," she groused before she stepped away, her eyes brimming with relief.

Molly could barely breathe. She was covered in mud and bruises. So was her son. She hugged him tight as rain lashed them.

Mo put a hand on her shoulder. "Better get into the car. I'm going to take you over to the hospital."

She nodded and followed him. She was fine, but she wanted to make sure Logan was all right. She sat in the back of the SUV with Logan, not wanting to let go of him.

"I'm sorry." She apologized to Mo again once Logan fell asleep, exhausted from his ordeal.

Skipper snored on the seat next to them, her head on

Logan's lap, smelling like wet dog. She didn't mind in the least. She could have hugged her. She'd saved their lives.

"You did what you thought was best in order to save your son." His gaze cut to hers in the rearview mirror. "But don't ever do it again. If you are in any kind of trouble, you call me first."

"Yes." She'd learned her lesson. "I wanted to trust you. I do trust you…" She bit her lip.

"What is it?"

"I'm a terrible decision maker. I've done so many stupid things over the years."

"I doubt that," he said mildly.

"You barely know anything about me."

"You have deep, dark secrets?" He sounded skeptical.

If only he knew… She squeezed her eyes together for a second. "My mother had affairs. A lot of them."

"You're not your mother."

"My father drank. I blamed her. We had a big fight one day. I told her we'd all be better off without her. She left. Instead of getting better, my father drank himself to death."

"Not your fault. He was the adult. You were the kid."

Oh, but he didn't know all of it. "Then I was…stupid with a guy a few years older than me. Got pregnant." She drew a deep breath, about to tell him something she'd never told anyone. "Mikey Metzner is Logan's father."

He'd been the most eligible bachelor in town, son of the owner of the wire mill. Now in jail for trafficking. She winced. A long silence stretched between them before she continued.

"I thought he'd be happy with the baby. I thought we'd be getting married. First he told me he didn't believe me that he was the father. Then he told me that if I repeated my dirty lies to anyone, he would make sure the baby was taken away from me. He has money to burn. He could hire every lawyer in the county."

Even now, if he ever decided he wanted a son. Even with him in prison, he could petition that custody be given to his mother. Grandparents had rights. With all his money, he could take Logan away from her, a fear she'd lived with for the past eight years.

"You were what, a teenager?" Mo asked, his tone clipped.

"Seventeen."

It sounded as if he was swearing under his breath, but she wasn't sure.

She didn't even want to know what he was thinking of her. That she was the village idiot, probably.

Which was so unfair. Because he was great, and she was completely in love with him.

Pitiful, really.

Epilogue

One week later

"If you want me to come get you, just give me a call," Molly said into the phone, standing in the middle of her foyer, looking out at the front yard where her three dogs were wrestling.

"No way, Mom," Logan said on the other end. "Aunt Grace needs me."

Yes, she was sure Grace made her son feel wanted. It was nice of her to offer to have him over for the birth of a foal that was coming into the world tonight. Logan was a tough little kid, but the kidnapping and escape from the mine had rattled him. He needed some new happy memories to push the bad ones away.

He'd been sticking to her like glue since the mine incident, even missed a day or two of school. And she'd been sticking to him, truth be told, not wanting to let him out of her sight. But she had to.

Even if she would be lonely tonight.

Or not, she thought as she saw Mo's SUV pull up her driveway. Her heart leaped.

"All right. Be very gentle and do whatever Grace tells you," she told Logan.

"Okay, Mom."

"I love you bunches."

"I love you, too."

Even if he thought he was too old to hold hands, he still thought saying *I love you* was okay. That was something. She was determined to enjoy what she could get before he reached the surly teenage years.

She hung up then went to let Mo in. She'd been locking her doors, a newfound habit.

They hadn't seen each other since the rescue. The team was working around the clock to track down a new clue Kenny provided them with, although Mo wouldn't tell her what it was.

He had asked whether Dylan had a friend named Coyote, but he wouldn't tell her who Coyote was, either. If her brother had known anyone like that, she knew nothing about it. Still, he did mention progress, which was nice to hear. She had a feeling his team was working on something big and it had nothing to do with policy recommendations.

"Hi." Mo came through the door, looking handsome and smelling like soap, probably fresh out of the shower.

The dogs were jumping all over him. He was handing out squeaky toys left and right. "I got some mighty big bones, too, in the car. Skipper gets double."

She'd missed him. Stupid. He was probably only here to read her the riot act over her stunt with Kenny. He'd said he'd understood, but then he hadn't come out to the ranch since.

She'd broken his trust. Of course, he was about to break her heart. She'd fallen for him and he would be leaving for the next step in his career as soon as his project here was finished.

She tried not to show how much the thought of that killed her. "How is work?" she asked as the dogs ran off with their toys.

"We're moving forward. Not as fast as we'd like, but it's something." He reached out and took her hand, sending her temperature up a notch.

It was ridiculous that all he had to do was touch her to make her go weak in the knees. He meant nothing by it. He'd seen her at her worst. He couldn't possibly want her.

So they'd had great sex. He'd probably had that with a lot of women. He probably wasn't dreaming of her every night, as she was dreaming of him.

"Sweet tea?" she asked by way of a distraction.

"Later," he said and kissed her.

Thank God was all she could think.

He tasted like prickly pear jelly.

He pulled away too soon. "I'm sorry I haven't come sooner. I missed you." He glanced toward the stairs. "Where's Logan?"

"Spending the night with Grace."

The grin that spread across his face was downright devilish. It sent her heart racing.

He dipped his head and this time kissed her deeper, claiming her. A blissful eternity passed before he pulled away again, with a satisfied look, and reached into his back pocket, pulledout an envelope and handed it to her. "A gift for you."

What? All she could think about was that kiss. She tore into the envelope impatiently then unfolded the papers, thumbed through them, stunned, her throat tightening.

Termination of parental rights. Signed by Mikey Metzner.

Mikey gave up his parental rights to Logan, forever and irrevocably. Logan was hers, only hers, and nobody could ever take her son away from her.

Moisture flooded her eyes. "How did you do this?"

"Offered him a nicer prison than the one where he was headed."

She flew into Mo's arms, and he gathered her against him, claimed her lips all over again. He explored her mouth, her face framed by his large hands, then kissed her eyes, planted more kisses down the line of her nose. He nudged her ear and nibbled his way down her neck, too.

When he backed her toward the kitchen counter, heat pooled at the V of her thighs. And she cringed.

"What is it?" he asked immediately.

She hung her head. "I'm embarrassed."

A puzzled look came over his face.

"I'm just like people say I am. Wanton and out of control." Her voice weakened as she admitted, "I've thought about this."

"And?"

"And I wanted it," she whispered.

He looked as pleased as peaches.

She swatted at his wide shoulder. "It's not normal. In the kitchen!"

"So you thought about the two of us? More than once?" He was watching her closely.

She gave a sheepish nod. "I'm a mother. I'm not supposed to think about naked men."

"How do you think people get the second and third kid?" His gaze searched her face. "So because of a few idiots who couldn't mind their own business, you locked your sensuality away."

It sounded kind of silly when he said it. Yet… "I'm completely out of control. I thought about you *a lot*. In worse places than the kitchen."

His eyes darkened with heat. "Go on. You thought about us where?"

She couldn't look at him. "Under the stars. Who does that? Maybe teenagers."

"The woman I love, that's who," he said and left her speechless. "Does that four-wheeler out in the garage have gas in it?"

"Sure."

He lifted her off the counter and took her hand. "Where are the keys?"

"What?" She felt the blood run out her face. Then it returned in a rush. And her body was suddenly tingling all over.

He didn't leave her time to hesitate, but drew her after him. He glanced at the keys by the back door, grabbed the right one.

They were in the middle of the fields by the time she half recovered, hardly able to believe that this was happening. He drove as if he was in a hurry. She had her arms tightly around his body, as much to hang on as because she liked the feel of him in her arms.

He finally stopped. They'd reached a high spot from where she could see her rolling fields in the moonlight, the stars bright above.

He shut down the engine then did some super move so he ended up with his back to the dashboard and her straddling him. She could feel his hardness through his jeans.

"You can't be serious."

But he did look serious. Very. "I want you."

She nodded weakly.

"I love you."

She had a hard time accepting that. "How do you know? It's too soon."

"When you know something is right, you don't have to think about it too much."

And she kind of understood what he was talking about,

because she felt the same way, as if Mo was right for her, just right, perfect.

But *she* wasn't perfect. Never had been.

Getting pregnant as a teenager was the least of it. She'd done worse things than that, much worse. She bit her lower lip. "I broke up my parents' marriage. I'm responsible for my father's death."

He took her hands. "How about you let them take some of that responsibility? I think you've punished yourself long enough."

She shook her head. "You sound like Grace."

"You have some damn smart people in your life. You should start listening to them," he said, making her smile.

A moment of silence passed between them.

"Have you ever heard from your mother?" He reached under her chin and lifted it.

She couldn't bear looking at him as she confessed, "A few years later she was beaten to death by a violent boyfriend." She swallowed hard. "If I didn't run her off—"

"No." He shook his head. "Your parents made their own choices. None of it was your fault. You were a kid."

His complete lack of judgment lightened some of the old heaviness inside her.

He rubbed his thumbs over her hands in a comforting gesture, then gave her a searching look, as if measuring her up for something. "I'm moving out to the ranch. I don't want you out here alone."

"Grace is alone."

"Ryder is with her as much as he can be. And Grace is an Army veteran. I want to be with you, and not just for your protection. But make no mistake, I will be protecting you. I don't think you're helpless, but I can't see you and Logan in danger. I'm just not made that way."

She stared at him.

"And I'm not coming just to protect you. I want to be with you."

Her heart turned over in her chest. "People will think I'm a total hussy if I shack up with you after barely knowing each other."

"People will extend us all courtesy, I believe."

Ha! "Why would they?"

"I'm about to become the town's favorite son. You'll be hosting social functions at my side. Can you handle the society pages?"

She had a hard time picturing herself anyplace else but in the gossip column at best. "I don't understand."

"I just talked my brother into building his new factory in Hullett. The town is about to see some seriously improved employment, I believe."

Her chin dropped. "You did that? Why?"

"I told you, I love you. I want to settle down here. What do you have to say about that?"

She swallowed. "The mind boggles."

HE GRINNED AT HER. "Not exactly what I wanted to hear. Let's try this again. I love you, Molly Rogers. What do you have to say about that?"

"I love you back," she said at last.

Warmth spread through his chest.

"Much better." He leaned forward and pulled her head to his.

But she held back. "What happens when you leave? I don't even know how long you'll be staying."

"I'm not going anywhere."

Hope filled her eyes. "What about that next level, the career move you wanted?"

"My father's dream. Here is the thing…" He rubbed his chin. "I see how you are with Logan. You just want him to be happy. When it comes right down to it, I think my father would have wanted that for me, too." He'd wanted to join the CIA to make his father's dream come true. While his father, if he was alive, would probably have wanted Mo's dream to come true.

And Mo's dream was Molly and a life with her and her son. "All I want is right here," he said. And then came the tricky part. "What I do... What if I can't really ever tell you about it?" Secrets could kill a relationship. He'd seen that in his line of business.

"Then I'll trust you that you have a good reason."

"Just like that?"

"I know you're working to stop people like Kenny. That's enough for me."

"You liked him. I'm sorry he betrayed you."

"He was only nice to me to be able to come and go at the ranch. He was hoping he could find the drugs without having to resort to drastic measures."

"You went on a date with him." A wave of cold jealousy washed over him even as he said the words.

"Worst date ever. I was thinking about you the whole time."

He kissed her.

If he lived to a hundred he wouldn't get tired of kissing her lips. He savored her thoroughly, distracted her from everything else. She might have fantasized about this, but it still made her nervous. First he made sure she was comfortable, then worked his way up to mindless passion.

He began unbuttoning her shirt, button by button, claiming with his lips every newly discovered inch of skin. Then the shirt disappeared. Her simple cotton bra made him smile. She wasn't given to vanity. But she was mind-blowingly sexy even without accessories.

Right now, even the cotton bra seemed like too much,

in fact. He reached around and unhooked it with more finesse than the last time, then bared her to his hungry gaze.

He covered one amazing breast with his hand, the other with his mouth. Her head dipped back, her lips slightly parting from pleasure. *Nothing* in the whole world was better than this.

She reached out to unbutton his shirt, timidly at first, then more boldly. Her fingers splayed over his chest. She seemed to enjoy touching him. Good. Because he suddenly felt as if he'd die if she took her hands away.

She stroked his heated skin gently, then more insistently, her soft core rocking against his hardness as she straddled him. He wanted to drag out the moment, the pleasure that nearly bordered on pain, and he did, but only for a few minutes before he reached the point where he needed more, where he needed it all.

He reached for the button on her jeans and she reached for his. A flurry of activity followed, which left them both breathing hard and naked. When he grabbed a foil pocket from his back pocket and took care of that, he drew her onto his lap again so she straddled him like before, but then he stayed still, letting her lower herself onto him when she was ready, wanting to let her set the pace even if it killed him.

When her moist opening touched against him, the searing pleasure stole his breath. But yet he held still. She braced her hands on his shoulders, her slim fingers kneading his flesh. Her perfect breasts, the most tempting fruit in the world, jutted forward inches from his face, the nipples hard pebbles.

She lowered herself slow inch by slow inch, while all he could do was hang on to her hips and drown in the pleasure she was gifting him. When he was fully sheathed, she stopped, looked into his eyes, hers wide with wonder. And then he gently rocked against her, smiling when her breath caught from the sensation.

He felt it, too, the building pressure.

She moved a little faster. So did he.

Then her hands tightened on his shoulders, her head falling back, a low, sexy groan escaping her throat. He leaned forward and took her hard nipple into his mouth, drew on it sharply while rolling her other nipple between his thumb and forefinger. He had no idea where he got that kind of coordination. His brain was pretty much melted.

But she appreciated the effort and with a cry went over the edge, tightening and pulsing around him. Which sent him flying.

Later, when they were trying to catch their breath, leaning against each other, he pushed the hair back from her face and kissed her.

"You're right," he said. "If I move to the ranch, town tongues will be wagging. I have a solution."

"You do?" she asked weakly, her face still glowing with pleasure, the most beautiful sight he'd ever seen.

He brushed his lips over her swollen mouth gently, then whispered the question in her ear. "Molly Rogers, would you marry me?"

* * * * *

HQ: TEXAS *is just heating up!*
Look for Dana Marton's next book, MY SPY,
on sale in October 2013. You'll find it
wherever Harlequin Intrigue books are sold!

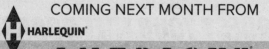

REQUEST YOUR FREE BOOKS!
2 FREE NOVELS PLUS 2 FREE GIFTS!

HARLEQUIN®

INTRIGUE®

BREATHTAKING ROMANTIC SUSPENSE

YES! Please send me 2 FREE Harlequin Intrigue® novels and my 2 FREE gifts (gifts are worth about $10). After receiving them, if I don't wish to receive any more books, I can return the shipping statement marked "cancel." If I don't cancel, I will receive 6 brand-new novels every month and be billed just $4.74 per book in the U.S. or $5.24 per book in Canada. That's a savings of at least 14% off the cover price! It's quite a bargain! Shipping and handling is just 50¢ per book in the U.S. and 75¢ per book in Canada.* I understand that accepting the 2 free books and gifts places me under no obligation to buy anything. I can always return a shipment and cancel at any time. Even if I never buy another book, the two free books and gifts are mine to keep forever.

182/382 HDN F42N

Name _____ (PLEASE PRINT)

Address _____ Apt. #

City _____ State/Prov. _____ Zip/Postal Code

Signature (if under 18, a parent or guardian must sign)

Mail to the **Harlequin® Reader Service:**
IN U.S.A.: P.O. Box 1867, Buffalo, NY 14240-1867
IN CANADA: P.O. Box 609, Fort Erie, Ontario L2A 5X3
**Are you a subscriber to Harlequin Intrigue books
and want to receive the larger-print edition?
Call 1-800-873-8635 or visit www.ReaderService.com.**

* Terms and prices subject to change without notice. Prices do not include applicable taxes. Sales tax applicable in N.Y. Canadian residents will be charged applicable taxes. Offer not valid in Quebec. This offer is limited to one order per household. Not valid for current subscribers to Harlequin Intrigue books. All orders subject to credit approval. Credit or debit balances in a customer's account(s) may be offset by any other outstanding balance owed by or to the customer. Please allow 4 to 6 weeks for delivery. Offer available while quantities last.

Your Privacy—The Harlequin® Reader Service is committed to protecting your privacy. Our Privacy Policy is available online at www.ReaderService.com or upon request from the Harlequin Reader Service.

We make a portion of our mailing list available to reputable third parties that offer products we believe may interest you. If you prefer that we not exchange your name with third parties, or if you wish to clarify or modify your communication preferences, please visit us at www.ReaderService.com/consumerschoice or write to us at Harlequin Reader Service Preference Service, P.O. Box 9062, Buffalo, NY 14269. Include your complete name and address.

HI13R

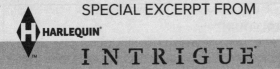
He reached for the glass of water on the nightstand and
stopped dead. The wide gold band on the ring finger of his
left hand glinted in the sunlight. He rubbed at his eyes, but
it didn't go away. He was married?

His head and stomach protested as he took in the strewn
clothing along with this new information.

No. Impossible. No way he'd forget his own wedding or
the inevitable events leading up to it. No way he'd marry a
stranger—and Ginger Olin, CIA operative, fit that description.
This had to be some ruse she'd invented to preserve her cover.

He couldn't make sense of the vague scenes flitting through
his mind. She owed him some answers. This time when he
pushed to his feet, he kept moving forward despite the sudden
tilt of the room. He was grateful when the wall kept him from
hitting the floor. He pounded a fist on the bathroom door. "Get
out here."

She opened the door and a steamy cloud of spicy vanilla scent washed over him.

"Oh, dear," she said with a sly smile as her gaze slid over his body like a touch. One long fingertip trailed across his jaw. "You're looking rough." She opened the door wider. "Come on in. A shower will fix you right up."

Was that a bit of Irish in her voice this morning? If so, was it real? He'd done a little investigating after their last meeting and knew she had a talent for accents.

She tucked herself under his arm, keeping him steady as she walked him past the long vanity. Something about the gesture felt familiar.

"Did you do this last night?"

"We can talk about last night when your head's clear." She eased back but didn't quite let go. "Steady?"

Barely. "Yes."

"Cold or hot?"

"Pardon?"

"The shower," she clarified, her eyes quickly darting down to his groin and back up again.

"Cold."

"All righty."

The secrets are only just starting.
Find out what happens next in
READY, AIM... I DO!
by USA TODAY *bestselling author*
Debra Webb

Available September 17, only from Harlequin® Intrigue®.